W9-CEE-641

Usborne Illustrated Ghost Stories

Usborne Illustrated Ghost Stories

Illustrated by
Jose Emroca Flores

Contents

The Phantom of Black Isle

"It would take a brave man or a fool to be out on a night like this," growled old Joshua, as the rain lashed the windows of the lighthouse lamp room.

His apprentice, Tom, looked out across the sea, where mountainous waves rose and crashed with deafening roars. Above them, bleak slate clouds swarmed across the sky like ragged demons.

Tom had been learning the trade of lighthouse keeper for almost a year now, but this was by far the worst storm he'd witnessed on Black Isle.

For a split second, the dazzling glare of the lamp went out, before immediately sparking back into life.

"Darned electrics," grumbled Joshua. "Never had this trouble with oil. You knew where you were with oil."

Tom smiled. Joshua had worked on Black Isle since the 1860s. The new century had brought many changes, and the old man sometimes struggled to accept them.

"Well if you're right, no one will need our lamp tonight, Joshua."

"No God fearing sailors, maybe," said Joshua with a grunt. "Only the likes of Jacob Gizard and his cronies come to grief on a night like this."

"Who's Jacob Gizard?" asked Tom.

"A stone-hearted villain who terrorized this coast one hundred years ago," Joshua replied.

Tom's eyes lit up. "A pirate?"

"That's too fanciful a name," spat Joshua. "Murderer I calls him. He plundered ships up and down this coast and killed those that got in his way."

"Did they ever catch him?" Tom asked.

Joshua gave a slight smile. "The sea caught up with him in the end. They say it was on a night like this he went about his dark business.

A storm whipped up and dashed his cutter, the *Sea Vixen*, to pieces on these very rocks. This was afore this lighthouse was built, y'see. The next morning, they found the wreckage washed up, but not a man jack of her crew. These waters handed out justice to Gizard and kept him for their own."

Tom shivered at the thought.

"That's enough yarning for one night," said Joshua. "You get along to your bunk. I'll wake you when it's your watch."

Despite the increased safety brought by the new electric lamp, Joshua insisted that he or Tom kept an eye on the machinery throughout the night.

"It only takes one spark, lad..." was his doom-laden warning.

Tom descended the winding stone steps to the tiny curved room that served as their sleeping quarters.

Despite the howling gale outside, Tom soon

sank into a deep sleep. His head was filled with thoughts of Gizard and his last fateful trip.

Tom imagined the *Sea Vixen* smashing into the razor sharp rocks below. He pictured the pirate struggling to stay afloat until all that was left was a bony, frozen hand poking above the waves. Somehow it seemed to be reaching out towards him…

"Look lively, lad!"

Tom woke with a start to find Joshua standing over him with a mug of steaming tea.

"What's the matter with you, boy?" he asked. "You're as white as a sheet. Storm's still raging," he added. "It'll be a long night…"

The next morning, the storm had fled with the dawn. The skies were clear and Tom felt a bracing breeze on his cheeks as he explored the rock pools that fringed the island.

Something glinting in the water caught his eye. Scrambling forward, he found a small golden coin wedged between two rocks. Tom used a sharp pebble to pry the coin free, and examined it. The head of King George the Third told him the coin must be around a hundred years old. A fanciful thought struck him. Could this be part of Jacob Gizard's treasure? Had it been brought ashore when the *Sea Vixen* broke up all those years ago?

Delighted with his find, Tom returned to the lighthouse. For a moment, he thought of showing the coin to Joshua. But he was worried that the old man might make him hand it over to the police or the revenue men who patrolled the local waters.

Under Tom's bunk was a small box he'd brought with him when he came to the island. It was here that he kept his collection of shells and other bits and pieces he'd found washed up on the beach.

Tom dragged out the box and took the coin from his pocket. Was it his imagination, or did it seem to glint just as brightly inside the dark room as it had done in the sunlight?

It shone with a light unlike any other Tom had ever seen. It was almost as if the coin itself were glowing.

Carefully, Tom wrapped the golden guinea in his handkerchief and placed it inside the chest.

That night, Tom took his turn on watch as usual in the lamp room. In contrast to the previous night, the sea was calm and quiet, almost eerily so. Surely no one would need Black Isle's guiding light tonight?

Tom let himself doze off for a few minutes. He was awoken by a low moaning sound. At first he thought it must be Joshua, grumbling about this and that as usual. But Tom was still all alone.

The moaning began to get louder, nearer… Had the sea not been so calm, Tom might have thought it was the wind. It was a mournful, pained sound, like a soul in torment.

As if from nowhere, a ship appeared on the horizon. Normally a vessel that far off would have been almost invisible at this time of night. But this was no ordinary ship. It was bathed from bow to stern in an ethereal golden glow, as if… as if…

Is it on fire? Tom gasped.

The ship sped ever closer and, as the moaning grew louder still, he realized there was something unnatural at work.

"Joshua!" he cried out in panic. "Joshua, come here quickly!"

Tom reached to pick up a telescope from a shelf behind him. He turned back, lifted the telescope to his eye and…

Nothing.

The ship had vanished as quickly as it had mysteriously appeared.

Joshua had staggered up the staircase. "What's all the hubbub, boy?" he panted.

How could Tom explain what he'd seen and heard, now that the sea was empty and the only sound was the breaking of the waves below? Joshua would think him crazy.

"Erm, nothing," mumbled Tom, red-faced. "I thought I saw... something. But I must have been mistaken."

Joshua snorted and went back downstairs, muttering under his breath.

Tom stood staring out to sea. Even if he had imagined the glowing ship, how had that unearthly moaning not woken Joshua?

He kept a sharp look out all night. But there was no sign of any vessels, let alone the mysterious glowing ship.

All next day, Tom could think of nothing but the previous night.

That evening, as he took over from Joshua in the lamp room, his stomach churned with anticipation of what might lie ahead.

The sea was rougher tonight. The waves rose to massive peaks, the sea continuously swirling and pounding. But, as the night wore on, nothing out of the ordinary occurred. So much so, that by midnight, Tom had once more allowed his eyelids to droop.

With a sharp crack, the light behind Tom went out and the lamp room was plunged into total darkness.

And then...

Just as before, a melancholy wailing filled the air, growing more insistent with each minute. The golden glow appeared far out to sea and began steadily making its way closer. The raging seas made the supernatural ship even more frightening than before, as it rose and fell, all the while racing towards the lighthouse.

Keeping his eyes fixed on the ship, Tom reached down for his telescope. In a single movement, he whipped the instrument to his eye. It took a few seconds for him to adjust to the violent glare of this closer view.

The ship was a cutter. On its deck Tom could make out a man dressed in the bicorn hat and knee britches of a hundred years ago. But his clothes were not the strangest thing about him.

The man's skin was a sallow, almost transparent yellow, which glowed in the night just like the vessel on which he stood.

As the ship carved its way ever nearer, Tom could make out every detail of the mariner's fearful face. His mouth was wide open, stretched beyond what seemed natural. The source of the terrible moaning became obvious. Tom stood transfixed by the man's horrible sunken eyes which seemed to be boring into his very soul. Then, to Tom's greater horror, the man raised his arm and pointed a skeletal finger straight at him. It was a bitterly cold night, but beads of sweat dotted Tom's forehead.

The ghastly figure twisted his hand and laid it open, palm up, as if waiting for something to be placed there.

'…the man raised his arm and pointed a skeletal finger straight at him.'

In that instant, fragments of what Tom had seen and heard in the past few days began to piece themselves together. As if to confirm his thoughts, the name plate of the ship became visible through the spray. '*The Sea Vixen*'.

Instinctively, Tom realized what he had to do. He fumbled his way to the top of the staircase in the dark, and edged his way down to the shared sleeping quarters.

Joshua lay asleep on his bunk. If the sorrowful moaning had miraculously left him undisturbed, Tom saw no point in trying to wake him. In any case, it was up to Tom to finish what he had unwittingly started.

He dragged the chest from under his bunk, tore open the lid and scrabbled around inside. Clutching the tightly folded handkerchief,

Tom raced back up the stairs to the lamp room.

The ship now seemed impossibly close to the lighthouse. Its golden glow almost matched the strength of the still extinguished lamp.

Shielding his eyes from the glare, Tom unwrapped the golden guinea from the handkerchief and went outside, onto the ledge of the lamp room.

Not daring to meet the terrifying gaze of the man he was sure was Jacob Gizard, Tom hurled the coin towards the ship.

The golden light flared up like an explosion and the next moment it was gone, along with the *Sea Vixen* and its sinister captain.

Tom slumped down in a heap and let out a long sigh of relief.

With a blaze of light, the sky was illuminated

once more. For a split second Tom's heart leaped at the frightful thought of the ship's return. But this light was a pure white beam that stretched out across the sea. The Black Isle lighthouse was back to normal.

Tom decided not to speak of the events of that night to Joshua. The old man would never believe him and, after all, there was no evidence to back up Tom's extraordinary experience.

Or was there?

A week later, along with their usual provisions, the local newspaper arrived by fishing boat from the mainland.

"Listen to this lad," said Joshua, as he skimmed through the paper after their supper that evening.

"'Divine rescue...'" Joshua cleared his throat. "'On the night of Thursday last, the steam cruiser, the Mary Anne, narrowly avoided disaster. On her way back from Le Touquet, the vessel found herself caught in a most dreadful storm and ended up many miles off course. For reasons unknown, the lighthouse on Black Isle was inoperative and the Mary Anne would surely have been dashed to pieces on the notorious rocks had it not been for the presence of a ship which emitted such a bright light, the captain of the steam ship took it to be a warning.'"

THE SOUTHERN EXPRESS, MARCH 20, 1905

DIVINE RESCUE

From our naval correspondent

On the night of Thursday last, the steam cruiser, the *Mary Anne*, narrowly avoided disaster.

On her way back from Le Touquet, the vessel found herself caught in a most dreadful storm and ended up many miles off course.

For reasons unknown, the lighthouse on Black Isle was inoperative and the *Mary Anne* woul surely have been dash to pieces on the notorio rocks had it not been f the presence of a sh which emitted such bright light, the capta of the steam ship took to be a warning.

Our artist's impression of the scen witnessed from the Mary Anne.

Smith and Jackson Ltd

Tom smiled. It seemed that Jacob Gizard had committed a good act at last, whether he intended to or not. Perhaps now the pirate might sleep soundly in the waters around Black Isle.

The Loyal Dog

In an old house, on the edge of a dark, smog-filled city, lived the Briar family: young Alfie, his mother and father, and Ruby, the family dog.

One cold October afternoon, when the wind was howling and the streets were empty, Alfie and Ruby were curled up by the fireplace. They were dozing quite peacefully when Alfie's mother burst into the room, waving several bulging files.

"Your dad just called," she said. "He has to work late but he's forgotten some important papers. He needs them for a meeting tomorrow. That man is so forgetful," she went on. "I'm surprised he remembers to put on clothes before he goes to work!"

Alfie glanced at the files, full of complicated diagrams, letters, and documents covered in official stamps. He could imagine his father panicking without them. He gave Ruby a big squeeze, then rose reluctantly to his feet.

"I'll take them," said Alfie, brushing a few dog hairs off his clothes. "His office isn't that far away. It shouldn't take too long."

"I don't know," his mother started. "It's getting dark out there, and I wouldn't want you running into any trouble. Perhaps you should take Ruby with you? Just in case."

"Ruby?" Alfie laughed, looking down at the tired old dog. Her breathing was slow and heavy, her coat looked worn, and he could just see her ribs poking out from under her skin.

"No," he decided. "Ruby needs her rest. She should stay here. I've been to Dad's office loads of times, I'll be fine."

"Then make sure you take your scarf," said his mother as Alfie slid on his shoes and found his coat. "It's chilly out there, and I don't want you catching a cold."

"Don't worry," Alfie replied, grabbing his scarf. "I'll be back soon." And he carefully squeezed the files into his satchel, slung the strap over his shoulder, and set off.

Outside, an icy wind was blowing. The sky was cloaked by a layer of murky brown smog, and what little daylight was left was quickly giving way to the yellow glow of street lights.

Alfie's breath puffed from his mouth in clouds as he walked. He paused for a moment to look back at the house, so snug and inviting. Then he buried his nose in his scarf, tucked his hands into his pockets, and set off – the heavy satchel bouncing up and down against his side.

As Alfie was making his way along, dreaming of his warm fireplace, he noticed something moving out of the corner of his eye.

At first, he thought nothing of it. He simply brushed it aside, thinking it was the flicker of the lights, or perhaps a rat scurrying in the shadows. But as he turned the corner onto a new street, there it was again – a glimpse of movement. He looked back in time to see something large and dark vanish between two buildings.

A shiver ran down his spine. "It's just my mind playing tricks on me," he said, snuggling deeper into his coat. He carried on, distracting himself with thoughts of *Riders of the Range* – a radio show set in the Wild West of America that was being broadcast later that night. By the time he reached the next junction, he was lost in daydreams of daring sheriffs and wily bandits.

That was when he heard it: the unmistakable sound of someone, or *something*, panting.

Alfie's heart started racing, and his palms were suddenly clammy.

"It's just the wind," he muttered. "I'm halfway to Dad's office already. And the sooner I get there, the sooner I'll be back home again."

But with every step he took, the panting grew louder, and louder, until he was certain there was something behind him. He turned sharply, not knowing what to expect, and saw...

...an empty street. There was no one around. The panting had stopped. There was no villain or monster waiting to pounce. Alfie sighed out his relief and carried on.

But as he strode ahead, he couldn't shake the uneasy feeling that he was being watched. Between every building, around every corner, he sensed movement, spied strange shadows, and heard the snuffling of some unseen creature. What he had thought was his mind playing tricks, now seemed very real.

Alfie picked up his pace, hoping to leave his fears behind. He avoided the shortcuts down dark alleys, and tried to stay as close to the street lamps as possible. But more than once, a low growl from the shadows had him change paths, and he soon lost his way entirely.

Finally, he found himself at a dead end, with a high fence before him and buildings on either side. Convinced he had been lured to his doom, his heart started hammering in his chest and sweat trickled down his back.

He stood stock still, holding his breath… but nothing happened.

Slowly, he retraced his steps, peeking around each corner, afraid of what might be lurking there, waiting to pounce. But this time he encountered no moving shadows, heard no ghostly noises. The wind, too, had died down, so that the only sound was the *tap, tap, tap* of his shoes on the paving stones.

By the time Alfie reached a familiar street,

he was feeling very foolish indeed.

"What will Dad think when I see him?" he wondered. He looked at his watch and saw how late it was.

In a panic, Alfie forgot all about the strange events of the evening. He clutched the satchel tightly to his chest and ran full-pelt in the direction of his father's office. He sprinted past silent buildings, bounded across uneven roads and skirted bare trees. Soon his feet were hurting and his breaths were coming sharp and short. "Almost there," he panted, encouraging himself.

And then, mid-sprint, a gigantic shadow spilled out from a side street in front of him. It stretched up and out, taking the shape of a beast with a terrifying head and cavernous mouth. With it came the soft *pit-pat, pit-pat* of paws on stone.

'...a gigantic shadow spilled out from a side street... a beast with a terrifying head...'

Alfie could feel his heart beating in his throat. All at once, his dad's office seemed farther away than ever.

"What do I do?" Alfie whispered, afraid to move forwards, but determined to reach his dad. All he could hear was panting, snuffling and the *pit-pat, pit-pat* of paws as the creature drew closer to the main street.

Alfie braced himself. He took a step back, lowered the satchel to the ground, and balled his hands into tight fists. "Come on, then!" he shouted, unable to keep the fear from his voice. "I'm ready for you!"

It arrived with the speed of some dark tornado, bounding around the corner so quickly that Alfie cried out in alarm. It leaped at him and a moment later, Alfie was on his back, pinned down by four large paws, while the tongue of a big, black dog slobbered all over his face. Not just any dog – *his* dog.

"Ruby?" shouted Alfie, in between wet dog licks. "What in the world are you doing here? You scared the life out of me!" He gently pushed the dog away, then rose to his feet and dusted himself off.

"So you're the one who's been following me all this time – and look at you! I haven't seen you with this much energy since you were a puppy."

Ruby wagged her tail, then jumped a few times and shook her glossy black coat.

"You look so young," said Alfie, incredulously, wondering if this really was his dog. The Ruby he had left dozing by the fireplace had eyes clouded with age, so that she could hardly see at

all. Yet here she was, staring clearly up at him.

Alfie jumped when a window swung open above them and a very red-faced man called out: "Will you please keep the noise down? I'm working up here, and all this shouting is making it very difficult."

"I'm sorry," Alfie replied. "My dog followed me and–"

"Dog? What dog?" the man interrupted.

"Why, Ruby of course." Alfie turned to point at the big, black dog. But Ruby was gone. "She was here a moment ago," he said, looking around for her.

Unimpressed, the man snorted and slammed the window shut.

Alfie searched around for Ruby, but couldn't see any trace of her. "Where could she have gone?" he wondered, baffled and amazed by how quickly and completely she had vanished.

"*Woof!*"

Startled, Alfie turned to see Ruby, sitting by his satchel, her head on her paws, looking as though she'd never been anywhere else.

"Where? How?" he began, before realizing he was unlikely to get a reply from a dog. He looked around, unsure whether to take Ruby home, or to continue to the office.

But when he glanced back at his dog, he found Ruby had disappeared again. So had his satchel. Another loud bark drew Alfie's attention to the end of the street, where Ruby was lolloping back in the direction of his house, the satchel hanging from her mouth.

"Hey!" Alfie called, running after the dog.

He could barely believe it. When he had left her, Ruby could hardly lift her own head, let alone carry a bag like that. Now she was off – running home and swinging it from side to side as if it were lighter than air. "Ruby, stop!" but the dog paid no attention.

He ran after her, hoping he could catch up with Ruby before she got too far ahead. But she was too fast, and Alfie was already tired from his fear-spurred sprint earlier. Before he knew it, they were back home. He felt his heart sink. His entire journey had been wasted.

Then he noticed Ruby, bounding up and down by the front door, the satchel lying discarded nearby. She whined and scratched at the door, and looked up at him with big, sad eyes, eager to get inside. Alfie sighed.

"Well, at least the house will be nice and warm," he said, picking up the satchel. He unlocked the door, swung it open, and immediately recoiled as the stench of something burning hit him. Before he could stop her, Ruby darted inside.

"Ruby!" Alfie shouted after her. Quickly, he covered his mouth with the sleeve of his coat, and followed her in.

The hallway was dark, and the only light he could make out was a bright red glow coming from the living room.

When he went to investigate, Alfie gasped. A log from the fireplace had somehow fallen from the grate and was now burning a hole in the floorboards.

Alfie snatched up the fire tongs, lifted the

log from the floor, and dropped it back onto the grate. But the floor was still smoking. So he whipped off his coat and started beating the floor with it until the fire was completely out. Then he opened all the windows to let the smoke out, and slumped to the ground, exhausted.

Alfie must have fallen asleep, because the next thing he knew, his mother was gently shaking him, her face lined with worry.

"Are you all right? What on earth happened?" she asked. "I just got home, the place stinks of smoke and your dad's files are still here."

As she made them both a mug of cocoa, Alfie explained everything that had happened that night, from the moment he left the house, to Ruby's sudden appearance, and his discovery of the fire.

When he was finished, Alfie's mother frowned. "You must be mistaken, dear. Ruby had some sort of seizure just after you'd gone, so I raced her to the vet."

She paused, sadness washing over her face. "...I'm so sorry, Alfie. When we got there, Ruby wouldn't wake up. She's gone. So you see, Ruby couldn't possibly have followed you."

There was silence as Alfie tried to understand what his mother was telling him. How could Ruby be gone? It wasn't possible – he had seen her with his own eyes. But then he remembered how young she had looked, and how mysteriously she had vanished.

"I know you probably won't believe me," Alfie said at last. "But Ruby came to find me tonight. She led me home to show me the fire. She was watching over us. Perhaps she always will."

The 4:15 Express

A few weeks before Christmas, 1865, my old friend Archie Jackson invited me to stay at his home, Claybridge Manor, in the east of England.

So one foggy December afternoon, I climbed aboard the 4:15 express train from London to Claybridge.

I'd just started reading when the door of my compartment opened and a tall, thin, elderly man entered.

I recognized him at once. His name was Horner, and he'd been a guest at Archie's house when I visited three years before. But he looked a lot older now. His skin was pale, his cheeks were sunken in, and there were deep lines etched across his forehead.

As he placed his coat on the rack above his seat, we exchanged glances.

"Mr. Samuel Horner, I believe?" I said. "My name is Paul Latimer, I'm a friend of Archie Jackson."

"Ah yes," Horner mumbled. "I thought I remembered your face."

"Are you on your way to Archie's house at

Claybridge too?" I asked.

"I may visit Claybridge Manor at some point over Christmas," he replied thoughtfully. "Mrs. Jackson is my cousin, as you may know. But at present I'm on a business trip."

"To Claybridge?"

"No, I get off at Blackbourne, the stop before. I'm a director of the East Anglian Railway Company and we're about to build a new line from Blackbourne to Penwood."

He started to go into a long, rather dull explanation of the difficulties involved in the project.

This, along with the stuffy compartment made my eyelids droop. I only woke when Horner suddenly raised his voice.

"...seventy-five thousand pounds, in cash!"

Waking with a start, and not entirely sure what he was talking about, I said cautiously, "That's a large sum."

"A large sum indeed," he said, nervously patting his breast pocket. "All the more so when I must carry it in person."

"In payment for...?"

"My dear sir," he sniffed impatiently, "haven't I been telling you for the past half-hour? The money is for Sir Thomas Trenchard's land, which lies on the route of our new railway line."

"Ah yes, of course," I nodded, pretending I'd simply forgotten. "So you said... And Sir

Thomas lives in Blackbourne?"

"The money is to be paid to his solicitor in Penwood. I'll hire a carriage at Blackbourne to take me there."

I was eager to change the subject which, apart from the large sum of money involved, didn't particularly interest me.

"Would you like me to pass any message to your cousin when I see her?" I asked.

Mr. Horner looked annoyed. "Well, you might ask her to have the chimney swept in my bedroom before my next visit," he said grumpily. "When I went up to dress for dinner the last time I was there, the room was full of smoke and the chimney was on fire."

I tried to hide a smile at the thought of this sight as the train slowed down on its approach into Blackbourne station.

At that moment, the carriage door opened and the guard entered.

"Ticket please," he said.

I handed over my ticket. The guard gave it a quick look, returned it and went on his way.

I turned to Mr. Horner in surprise. "He didn't ask to see yours."

"They never do," he said. "I'm a director of the line, my face is known and I travel for free."

"Blackbourne! Blackbourne!" cried the station porter as we pulled into the platform.

Mr. Horner tugged on his coat. "Good evening, Mr. Latimer."

"Good evening," I said, holding out my hand.

But he either didn't notice, or chose to ignore me. Instead he stepped out onto the platform and merged with the departing passengers.

Leaning forward to look out of the window, I felt something beneath my foot. Stooping down, I picked up a leather cigar case with the initials S.H. Assuming it had fallen from Horner's coat pocket, I sprang out of the carriage and approached the porter.

"Have I got time to return this to my friend before the train goes?" I asked breathlessly.

"If you're quick, sir," he replied. "Just a minute and a half."

Calling out my thanks, I rushed along the platform, trying to find Horner in the crowd.

Then I saw him, halfway along the platform, deep in conversation with a younger man in a heavy overcoat. He was a stout fellow with fair hair and a bushy beard.

I quickly dodged my way around the passengers between us, aware that my train would be leaving at any moment. Just as I drew close to him and his companion, I stumbled over a large bag.

When I looked up, I was amazed to discover that Horner and the other man had vanished. I had only looked away for a split second, but in that time they had disappeared into thin air.

I spun around as I felt the hand of the porter on my shoulder.

"If you want this train, you must jump aboard now sir."

"There were two gentlemen standing here just a moment ago," I panted. "Did you see where they went?"

"I saw no gentlemen, sir," he said. "Now please, you must hurry."

Grinding my teeth in frustration, I ran back to the train as it pulled out, and only just managed to scramble back into the carriage.

For the rest of the journey, I puzzled over this mysterious event. It was like a magic trick. One moment Horner had been there, the next he was gone. There had been no door nearby, no staircase... Just a bare platform.

What could have happened?

I was still wondering about it when Archie greeted me at Claybridge Manor.

My old friend directed me to my room and I dressed for dinner, all the while thinking about what had occurred earlier. I was so distracted that I only just had time to introduce myself to Archie's wife and my fellow house guests before we sat down to eat.

The conversation was rather boring and eventually stopped altogether as the main course arrived. I decided to liven things up by telling the story of my train journey.

"By the way, Archie," I began, "I came down today with a friend of yours. He said he might visit over Christmas. As a matter of fact he's a relation of yours, Mrs. Jackson."

"Really?" said Archie's wife. "Who?"

"It was your cousin, Samuel Horner."

Archie laid down his knife and fork. His wife looked at me in a strange, startled way. I carried on, undaunted.

"He asked me if you could have the chimney swept in his room before his next visit. He was worried about getting covered in soot again."

As the words left my lips, I realized I had said

something wrong. For at least two minutes, there was a dead silence across the table. Eventually the hush was broken by a fellow guest, who started talking about a play he had seen recently.

After dinner, I went up to Archie. "What did I say wrong, earlier?" I asked quietly.

"You mentioned Samuel Horner," he said.

"What was wrong with that? I'd seen him less than two hours ago."

Archie looked at me intently. "Are you absolutely sure it was him?"

"Of course," I said. "But why should that surprise you?"

Archie glanced around and then dropped his voice to a whisper. "Because Samuel Horner disappeared three months ago with seventy-five thousand pounds of the Railway Company's

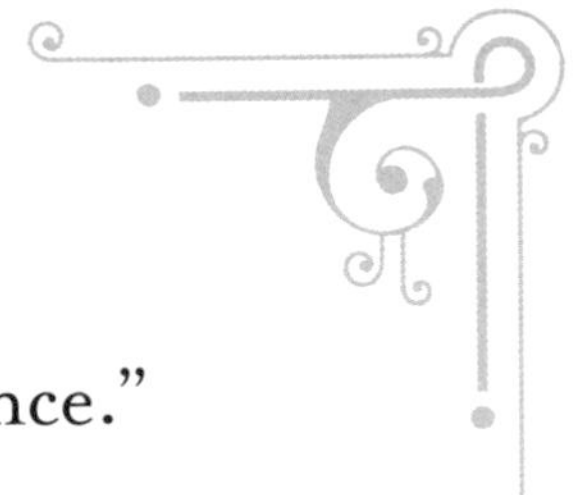

money and has never been heard of since."

I could hardly believe what I was hearing.

Archie went on. "You must have mistaken this man for Horner."

"Impossible," I insisted. "I recognized him immediately from his visit here before. He talked to me about his work for the Railway Company, not to mention his stay at Claybridge and that business with the chimney. How could anyone else know all that?"

"But what has he been doing for the past three months?" wondered Archie aloud. "How did he look?"

"Older, paler and more nervous since the last time I saw him," I replied.

"Hardly surprising for a man on the run."

"So why has he come back?" I asked. "And

why did he make such a point of telling me about the money?"

Archie thought for a moment. "Perhaps he's been hiding out in the countryside, feeling guilty about what he's done," he suggested. "At last, he's decided to return the money and hand himself over to the police."

I thought this was unlikely, but couldn't offer another solution.

"If only you had some proof," sighed my host.

"But I do!" I cried. "Follow me."

I led Archie to my bedroom and produced the leather cigar case from my coat pocket.

"It certainly looks like the one he uses," said Archie, after I'd explained how I came by it. "And it does have his initials on the side."

"This at least proves I didn't dream the whole thing," I said.

"We shall go to Blackbourne station tomorrow," declared Archie. "Someone there must have seen Horner."

"Thanks," I said gratefully. "It will be a weight off my mind to clear up this whole thing."

So it was that the next morning Archie and I arrived on the platform at Blackbourne station.

Sadly neither the station-master, nor the porter, nor any of the other staff had any memory of seeing Horner the previous evening. In fact, they all thought it unbelievable that the man would dare show his face anywhere on the line ever again, given that his face was so familiar and his crime so great.

On asking about the guard who had inspected my ticket, we discovered that his name was Grant and that he was due in on the next express train, which would stop at Blackbourne for ten minutes.

When he arrived, we started by asking if he remembered me and could recall checking my ticket the previous evening.

"Why, yes sir," he said.

"And did you recognize the man who was with me?" I asked.

"What man would that be, sir?" replied Grant. "You were alone."

I was shocked. "The man sat directly opposite me," I insisted. "Mr. Horner of the East Anglian Railway Company. You must have seen him."

"I'm afraid I saw no one, sir," declared Grant. "Beg pardon sir, my time's up."

With a touch of his cap, he boarded the engine and the train glided slowly out of the station.

Frustrated by our lack of success, Archie and I returned to Claybridge Manor.

A week later, I was surprised to receive a letter from the East Anglian Railway Company, asking me to attend a meeting with their directors at their London office. I guessed that they had heard about my investigation and wanted to learn more.

On arrival, I was led into a grand room where a dozen stern-looking gentlemen were seated around a large table.

The chairman and his fellow directors began

to question me about the events of that night, the 4th of December. I told the story of my train journey, at one point showing them the cigar case, which they all recognized.

After I had finished, they called for Grant the guard, who gave his own account. Once again, he swore that I had been alone in the compartment and that he had not seen Mr. Horner.

The chairman turned to me once more.

"You have heard Grant's statement," he said seriously. "It doesn't match yours."

"I can only repeat myself," I replied. "I was with Horner until he left the train at Blackbourne. I even saw him walk along the platform where he was met by a friend."

"Ah! Can you describe this person?" asked the chairman.

I thought back. "He was stout… fair-haired and with a bushy beard. He wore a heavy overcoat and I'd say he was around thirty-five to forty years old."

But the chairman seemed uninterested in my description. Instead, he talked with his colleagues and then questioned Grant about his duties that day. It became clear that they were beginning to suspect that Grant and Horner had been working together somehow.

The chairman turned to a man by the door. "Ask Mr. Crabbe to bring in the list of all the guards on duty that day."

A moment later, Crabbe entered the room carrying a large book under his arm.

As soon as I saw him, my heart leaped. I sprang to my feet and pointed a quivering finger in his direction. "That's the man Horner met on the platform!" I cried.

Gasps of surprise filled the air.

The chairman fixed Crabbe with a steely glare. "Where were you on the evening of the 4th of December, Crabbe?" he asked.

"Here sir," he replied softly. "Where else should I be? Ask Mr. Law."

The chairman gestured to a man opposite him who was obviously Crabbe's boss. He consulted some papers and agreed that Crabbe had been in the London office until late that night.

"In fact," added Mr. Law, "Mr. Crabbe has not been away from the office since he had two weeks off three months ago."

"It appears that you're mistaken, Mr. Latimer," sighed the chairman. "There seems little point in pursuing this matter."

"Three months ago!" I exclaimed. "That's exactly when Horner went missing. There must be a connection."

"You can't prove anything!" croaked Crabbe, sounding desperate.

"I know what I saw," I cried to the chairman. "Crabbe was definitely on Blackbourne station with Horner."

I turned to see Crabbe, looking as white as a sheet, his lips trembling, rushing frantically to the door.

Leaping from my seat, I bounded across the room and grabbed him by the shoulders, holding him back.

"Let me go!" he cried. "I don't know what you're talking about. I'm innocent."

'...I bounded across the room and grabbed him by the shoulders, holding him back.'

"That remains to be proved," declared the chairman. "I shall put the matter in the hands of the police. As for your accomplice, Horner..."

"I had no accomplice," cried Crabbe, breaking down. "Only have mercy upon me. Make the police spare my life and I'll confess all. I didn't mean to harm him!"

"Has murder been committed?" asked the chairman, horrified.

"Not murder," shrieked Crabbe, falling to his knees. "I thought I'd stunned him. I never meant to kill him. It was an accident – not murder!"

Crabbe then confessed that he'd met Horner from the train at Blackbourne, taken him along a deserted country lane on the way to Penwood, and struck him down. He had planned to escape to America with the seventy-five thousand pounds.

But on discovering that he'd killed Horner, he realized that nowhere in America would be safe for a wanted murderer.

The chairman looked at Crabbe gravely. "Then you forged the records showing you were here in London on the 4th of December?" he asked.

"Oh no, sir," replied Crabbe, sounding genuinely puzzled. "The events I've just described took place on the 11th of September. Mr. Horner's body has lain in a ditch by the Penwood road ever since that terrible day."

I was stunned.

I suppose it was possible that Horner's cigar case had fallen from his pocket on the September evening he journeyed to Blackbourne. It was just possible that it had remained on the floor of the selfsame compartment I had occupied in December.

But it did not, and never shall explain, how I shared a railway journey with a man who had been dead for twelve weeks.

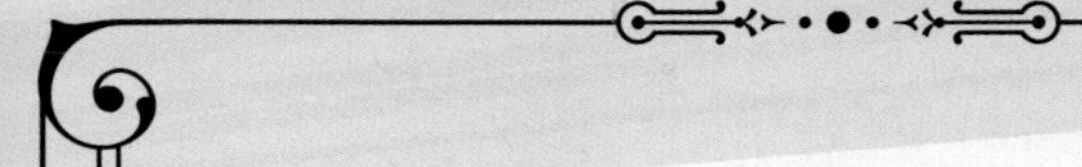

The Lost Legion

"Only two weeks more, and I'll be home," sighed James as he climbed into bed and pulled up the covers.

His brother and sister had come down with a fever three weeks ago, and he had been packed off in the swiftest carriage to stay with his Great Aunt Caroline, so he didn't catch it too.

Great Aunt Caroline lived in a big old house on the edge of a windswept moor.

She was rather deaf, had white hair tucked under a lace cap, and a great many wrinkles.

She had tried to be kind to him, but she was so old and, as she lived alone (except for her servants), she was not used to any kind of disturbance. She sat in her high-backed chair in the front room and read all day from great leather-bound history books.

She expected James to read all day too, but the books were heavy and full of dull facts, with hardly any pictures. Besides, he missed his brother and sister and the rough-and-tumble games they played together at home.

James lay in the dark, listening to the sounds of the old house. Even from his room at the end of the corridor, he could hear the slow ticking of the clock in the downstairs hall. A screeching whine and then a clang. That was the iron gate, swinging on its hinges.

But there was also a soft, steady pattering – or maybe, yes, more like thudding – that James couldn't explain. He had heard it last night too, but tonight it seemed stranger than ever. If he hadn't known better, he would have said it was footsteps, all marching in time. They didn't get any closer or any further away, they just tramped, tramped, tramped.

The more James thought about it, the odder it seemed. He had to find out what it was.

Moonlight filtered faintly in at the windows, casting a dull light around the room. He climbed out of bed and headed down the great wooden staircase, treading as softly as he could. Near the bottom step, the strange noise was clearer and closer, and sounded even more like footsteps – an entire army of them, marching steadily.

James's scalp prickled and he stayed very still, suddenly afraid. But there was no one there. Apart from a few faint shadows cast by the moonlight, the front hall was empty. James stood silently, peering into the gloom, and the rhythmic marching grew softer and softer, until it faded away.

James tiptoed back upstairs, wondering if he had imagined the whole thing. Back in bed, he burrowed beneath scratchy blankets. He was still puzzling over it as he drifted off to sleep.

The next night, he lay in the dark again, listening... At first, there was nothing out of the ordinary: the moaning wind, the creaking gate, and the distant ticking of the clock. But then

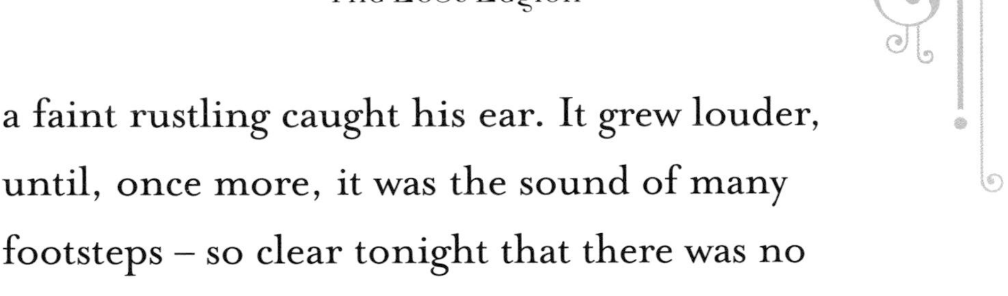

a faint rustling caught his ear. It grew louder, until, once more, it was the sound of many footsteps – so clear tonight that there was no mistaking it.

James started to go downstairs, peering into the hallway. Tonight, something was different. The air seemed thicker and darker, as if the hall were filled with a gloomy fog. It was moving slightly, like mist seeping up from the ground.

Reaching the last step, James stopped dead. He had caught a glimpse of something through the swirling mist – something that gleamed like polished metal in the moonlight and was moving steadily, in time to the footsteps.

The mist started clearing and now he could see men striding past him. Glints of metal shone from their clothes, and they were marching steadily across his path.

They were all dressed the same, with pleated tunics swinging against their knees, their chests bound with leather and metal. Short swords hung from their belts, their feet wore leather sandals and each man carried a spear.

As the men reached the misty shadows at the end of the hall, they disappeared. More figures followed, emerging from the gloom on the other side, where James knew a wall ought to be. It was as if the house wasn't even there.

The men's faces were set and grim under gleaming helmets, and they looked straight ahead. None of them seemed to notice James, so he simply stood there, too shocked to move.

Just as he thought the line would go on forever, there came a figure on its own, with

'Glints of metal shone from their clothes... they were marching steadily across his path.'

no one behind. This man seemed smaller and slighter than the rest, and his eyes moved from side to side, as if scanning for danger.

As he passed James, his eyes flickered in alarm and he paused mid-stride, but he recovered quickly. "*Adiuva! Adiuva nos!*" he said in a low, urgent voice.

Before James could do anything, the man headed into the shadows and vanished. James stood with his mouth open, trying to take in what he had just seen. The footsteps grew fainter, until they, and the mist, faded away altogether. The shadowy hall was as empty as usual.

James went back to bed, his mind whirling with images of the ghostly soldiers. The words the man spoke were not English, but something about them seemed familiar.

His dreams were filled with clashing swords and shouts, and he woke with a phrase echoing in his head: "Help! Help us."

Of course! That was what the figure had said – in Latin. So had he seen a *Roman* army? But how could he possibly help them? History was not his strongest subject, though there was always Great Aunt Caroline and her books...

It took a huge effort, but he held in his questions until after breakfast. When Great Aunt Caroline was seated as usual in her tall chair, he stood in front of her, a little nervous, and cleared his throat. "Great Aunt Caroline," he began, and then faltered as she raised her eyes from her book and fixed them sternly on his face. He forced himself to go on.

"I expect you've read a great deal about the

Romans. When they lived here. Men in helmets and so on…"

He trailed off, knowing that he sounded ridiculous. But, to his relief, Great Aunt Caroline was smiling.

"The Reverend Gaskell and myself conversed on that very topic not two weeks ago," she said. "Such a learned man. He personally began the excavations at the Roman camp on the hill yonder." She gestured towards the window. "It was the headquarters of the Seventeenth Legion, you know."

James certainly didn't know, but he nodded to show he was paying close attention.

"I came across a reference to it only the other day…" Great Aunt Caroline heaved herself from her chair and reached for a leather-bound

volume, leafing through the pages.

"Yes, here it is: 'The Seventeenth Legion, widely famed for its courage and victories, on the fifteenth day of August marched out from its camp to put down a rebellion among the local tribes. It is said the soldiers departed along the old north road, but this was the last news to reach Rome. They were never seen again.'"

Great Aunt Caroline shut the book and looked hard at James. He stared back, still taking in the story. Was that why the soldier had asked him for help? Was he meant to find some trace of the lost legion? He didn't know what else he could do.

"A remarkable coincidence," Great Aunt Caroline observed, "that it is the fifteenth day of August today. The old north road actually passed this way. In fact, Reverend Gaskell once suggested that it passed through my grounds – that the front hall of this house was built over it."

James started in surprise. But Great Aunt Caroline hadn't finished. "It is a fine day. I will order the carriage. The first time I visited the camp I was around your age. I liked to imagine the place was filled with the ghosts of the departed legionaries."

James glanced at her, wondering how much she knew. But she had turned away and was already walking to the door.

It was only a short drive to the camp. James tumbled eagerly out of the carriage, then stood still, looking around in disappointment. The old headquarters of the Seventeenth Legion was only a field, with a few stubs of stone sticking up out of the grass.

Great Aunt Caroline was already pointing out the features.

"Over there," she said, gesturing with her stick, "is the northern gate, by which the troops left that fateful August day, never to return."

James ran over, pausing by the remains of the gatehouse and gazing along the old road. He could just make out where it ran across the lonely moor, past Great Aunt Caroline's house and then on, into the hazy distance. Although the day was warm, he felt the hairs on the back of his neck stand up. Somehow he knew that, to help the soldiers, he needed to follow them along that road.

Hearing his great aunt call, he turned to go and his foot struck something hard. He winced and bent down to rub his toe, noticing that he had dislodged a large piece of stone. As he picked it up, a shiver ran through him, making him tingle all over. He had the strongest feeling that the stone was important. One side was smooth and had markings carved into it. It took some rubbing to get the dirt out, but his heart beat faster as he read the inscription: LEGIO XVII – the Seventeenth Legion.

James stumbled over to his great aunt, clasping the stone.

"I am glad to see you are interested in your Roman history," she said, "but this fresh air is tiring your old Aunt. We will go home now."

The day seemed endless. The moment Great

Aunt Caroline went to her room after supper, James collected the stone, crept to a side door being careful to avoid the servants, and quietly let himself out.

The summer sun was low in the sky, but that made it easier to see the faint line of the old north road stretching across the moor ahead. It felt eerily empty and quiet, as if waiting for something to happen.

A cold breeze blew, and rooks flapped and cawed around a stunted oak tree further up the road. James noticed with some alarm that the sun was sinking fast. He didn't like the idea of being up here alone in the dark.

As he neared the oak tree, the stone suddenly felt dreadfully heavy and he had to put it down. He lowered it to the ground and again the strange tingling flowed through him. It seemed the stone wanted to be there.

James sat down for a moment, wondering what he should do next.

Just then, a rook flew down from the tree and landed close by. With a *cawwww*, it started tugging at a stick half-buried among the roots of the tree, before flying off.

James grabbed the stick and pulled. It came loose, bringing up a shower of mud, pebbles... and something else, something small and pointed. James rubbed it, and was amazed to see an arrowhead, rusty after centuries in the soil, but still sharp.

Looking into the hole left by the stick, he saw a gleam of something rounded and creamy-white. He began to brush the mud from it, feeling the familiar tingling shiver pass through his body. The next moment, he pulled back in horror as he recognized the shape of a human skull.

He crouched there for a second, his heart thumping wildly, unable to take his eyes from it. The face of the last soldier, the one who had spoken to him, floated into his mind.

It seemed to hover above the skull, and in that moment James knew what had happened to the Seventeenth Legion. The local tribes it had been sent to quell had ambushed the men here, on the road, and left not a single soldier alive to tell the tale.

The last gleam of the setting sun flashed across the bleak moor and a gloomy mist began rising up from the ground around him.

As he watched, the mist flickered and took

shape, and he was surrounded by the dim figures of armed men, bright helmets gleaming faintly.

They were all facing him, their arms raised in a silent salute – and there, at the front, was the smaller, slighter figure who had spoken to James only the night before.

His lips were moving again, and James heard the words, "*Ave atque vale,*" as faint as a whisper.

Then, as the sun dropped out of sight, the misty figures shimmered and disappeared.

"Hail and farewell," translated James to himself, as he carefully patted the soil back over the skull and set the carved stone on top.

At long last, the graves of the Seventeenth Legion were marked – they weren't lost any more.

James started back along the road, whistling to himself in the twilight. He wondered what Great Aunt Caroline would make of it all, but he suspected that he wouldn't ever have the nerve to tell her.

Bring Out Your Dead

The Leech Investments Building stood tall and stately in the heart of London. But while the old stone building was much-loved, the same could not be said of its owner, Robert Leech.

"I'm not interested in excuses," he barked, from the comfort of his luxurious office on the sixth floor. "I'm interested in results."

Harold Thompson trembled in his seat, as his boss yelled at him.

"Your department hasn't made a profit for the third month in a row," Leech ranted. "I run a business, Thompson, not a charity."

"I'm sorry Mr. Leech," stammered Thompson, "But you see, my wife hasn't been well lately, and my three children are–"

"I don't care about your private life," sneered Leech. "I'm only interested in making money. If you can't do that, you're of no use to me. Leave your security pass with Ms. Rivers on your way out."

"I don't understand," began Thompson.

"Then let me make myself plain."

Leech stood up and pointed to the door. "You're fired! And I have an appointment with a newspaper reporter in five minutes, so get out."

With his head bowed, Thompson crept out of Leech's office.

Inconvenient though it was to have to dismiss an employee, Leech had to admit it gave him a pleasant feeling of satisfaction.

For a moment, he paused to admire his 17th century painting of what was now the Leech Investments Building.

The property had been in the family since his father started the company nearly fifty years ago. Leech had always admired the old man's business skills. He'd built the company up from nothing and devoted his whole life to it. Months would go by without Robert even seeing his father, such was his dedication to the business. He never let anyone stand in his way, and crushed his rivals.

It was a pity Father went soft after Mother walked out, Leech thought. The old man had seemed so full of regrets at the end. But why? He was rich and powerful. Surely that was all that mattered?

"Wonderful picture," said a voice behind him. "By van der Heyden isn't it?"

Leech turned to see a short, elderly man with large spectacles, wearing a long overcoat and an old-fashioned trilby hat.

"Who are you?" snapped Leech.

"I've come to ask a few questions, if I may?"

Leech shrugged. *Hmm, he doesn't look much like a reporter. And how inefficient of Ms. Rivers not to announce him. I shall have to have words with her...*

The reporter held out his hand, but Leech ignored it, and pointed to the chair opposite his desk. Leech never shook hands. It was an unhygienic habit. One never knew what *ordinary* people had been doing.

"Well, what do you want to know?" he asked briskly, settling himself in his shiny swivel chair. "I'm a busy man. Can't spend all my time chatting with the press."

The reporter took off his hat and carefully placed it on Leech's antique desk. Leech shot him a disapproving look, but decided to ignore the lack of respect. He wanted this little man out of his office as soon as possible. He had money to make.

"Just a character profile, really," said the reporter. "We've been following your progress for some time."

"*We*?"

The reporter smiled. "My employers and I. We're particularly interested in your approach to business and your methods."

"Invest cheaply, sell for a profit," Leech declared proudly.

"Ah yes, your investments," the reporter said softly. "Nuclear power plants with poor safety records. Diamond mines that pay their workers a pittance for 12-hour shifts. A factory where children as young as five are made to work..."

Leech's eyes flashed with anger. "All my investments are perfectly legal," he retorted.

"And what about the employees?" asked the reporter. "What about the *ordinary* people who work for you?"

Leech flinched, slightly surprised at hearing his own phrase. "If you've only come here to insult me, I suggest you leave," he said, standing up quickly.

"I can't persuade you to reconsider the way you live?" asked the reporter.

"What are you talking about?" asked Leech.

"We just wanted to give you a chance to change your ways, before we... act," said the reporter.

"Is this an interview or a trial?" asked Leech. "I've had enough of this. Get out!"

The reporter stood, picked up his hat and moved to the door, pausing briefly to look at the painting again.

"It really is striking," he observed, "and, I believe, painted just after this building was completed in 1670, barely three years after the Great Fire of London."

"I am aware of that fact," said Leech tersely. "I own this building."

"A terrible thing, fire," added the reporter.

"Not in that case," said Leech. "Didn't it help end the Great Plague?"

"One hundred thousand people died in that plague," said the reporter. "'Bring out your dead!' Isn't that what Londoners used to cry?"

"I believe so," replied Leech, impatiently ushering the talkative man to the door.

"Horrible to think that so many bodies ended up buried in plague pits, all over London," the reporter went on. "Did you know they sometimes find the remains of the pits under old buildings like this one?"

"I'm not interested," said Leech.

"Of course not," said the reporter. "After all, they were just *ordinary* people too."

"I shall be having words with the editor of your paper," snarled Leech. "Who did you say you worked for?"

The old man paused. "The er... *Examiner*," he replied with a smile. With a tip of his hat, he left the room.

Leech felt flustered. He wasn't used to feeling

flustered. He was about to take his annoyance out on his secretary, when she knocked and entered.

"Excuse me, Mr. Leech," she said. "I've just had a call from the reporter. He's had to cancel I'm afraid."

"What are you talking about?" said Leech, confused. "He just left. Didn't you see him?"

Ms. Rivers looked puzzled. "I didn't see anyone, sir," she replied. "The last person to leave your office was Mr. Thompson."

Leech couldn't understand it. He sent his secretary away, and slumped in his chair, lost in thought. The man had gone out. He'd seen him leave. Ms. Rivers must have left her desk for a moment, that was it. No other explanation.

He spent the rest of the day looking at profit forecasts. This usually cheered him up. But not today. Try as he might, he couldn't shake the thought of that strange little man. *Well, he can write what he likes for his paper,* thought Leech. *I don't care in the least.*

It was nearly midnight by the time he finally stopped work. As usual by that time, he was the only one in the building. There wasn't even a security guard. Leech had decided they were a waste of money. Paying people to sit on their bottoms all night? Ludicrous! His new electronic locking system was far more efficient. People had complained that it ruined the look of the old building. Too bad.

Leech was putting some papers in his briefcase when he felt a chill run up his back. How curious. It was an otherwise mild night.

As he shivered, he heard something ringing.

For a second, he thought it was the fire alarm, but as it got louder, he realized it was a hand bell, pealing in a slow rhythm.

There must be someone else in the building... Burglars! But why would they draw attention to themselves by ringing a bell?

Then came a voice. A low, moaning, wretched, miserable voice.

"Bring out your dead! Bring out your dead!"

Leech's pulse sped up. If this was that reporter's idea of a joke...

At that moment, there was a strange, shimmering movement on the floor of the office. At first, it looked like a dark stain, gradually spreading out, larger and larger. Then, up through the middle of the stain came the head of a bearded man, his skin covered in dark red blotches, his eyes bloodshot and blank.

Leech stared in terror as the man, dressed in a tattered jerkin and breeches and looking vaguely transparent, rose up before him.

The man fixed his awful, dead gaze on him. "Master Robert Leech?" he said calmly.

Leech, rooted to the spot with fear, could only grunt in reply.

The man looked at Leech's richly furnished office. "You truly live in fine style," he said. "A pity your servants do not fare so well."

"I d-don't know what you mean," stuttered

Leech. "Who are you? How did you get in here? What do you want?"

"I come in search of change."

Leech was confused. "You want to change?"

"It is not I who must change, but YOU!" spat the man, pointing a bony finger at the figure before him, cowering behind his chair. "Give up your grasping ways. Do right by those who serve you. Or suffer the consequences."

Leech reached for his phone. "I'm calling the police," he said, his voice trembling. But there was no signal.

"No officer of the Watch may save you now," said the man, the faintest hint of a smile playing around his cracked lips. "Repent or you will face eternal damnation."

And then, to Leech's horror and disbelief,

the man floated forward, his feet hovering just above the ground, his arms outstretched.

"Don't touch me!" yelled Leech, backing away in dread. "You're filthy."

The man stopped. "'Tis but the plague," he said with a grin, before continuing towards his victim.

"Keep away, keep away!" Leech screamed, dashing around his desk to the door and fleeing his office.

The ghost made no attempt to follow. "Run, then," he laughed. "Run like a startled rabbit. You won't escape us."

Us? thought Leech, as he raced down the corridor in panic. Were more of these creatures lying in wait for him?

His question was soon answered.

'Up through the floor came the ghosts of men, women and children.'

Up through the floor came the ghosts of men, women and children. All of them wore the dirty, ragged clothes of 17th century workers. Each had deathly white skin, covered in red blotches. Through their ragged sleeves, Leech could see pus-filled blisters under their armpits. He shuddered, feeling sick.

He darted around the phantoms as they reached out to touch him. Sweat pouring down his face, he headed for the staircase.

"Repent or perish!" wailed the ghosts, floating towards him. "Change or be haunted forever!"

"Never!" growled Leech, through gritted teeth. He tugged open a door and hurtled down the stairs. *Only six floors up. Surely I can outrun them?* He ran so fast it felt as if he were falling headfirst.

Panting for air, he finally reached the door

to the lobby. His hands shaking, he took his electronic door card from his pocket and swiped it in the lock. Nothing happened. Again and again he tried, struggling to keep a grip on the plastic with his clammy fingers. It was no use.

The familiar peal of bells filled the air and the terrifying spirits loomed up through the floor all around him.

"Repent!" they moaned. "Repent!"

The fire exit, thought Leech. *That's not electronic.*

Scuttling past his pursuers, he ran along a passageway. Up ahead he could see the fire exit door. All he had to do was push the bar and he was free. He was only feet away, when the bearded man who had menaced him in his office materialized between Leech and his only chance of escape.

Leech fell to his knees in despair. He'd been within touching distance of the fire exit...

Fire! That's it. If fire was enough to finish the plague before, let's see how these wretched peasants cope with it.

He scrambled through a side door into a maintenance room. Lining the shelves were cleaning products of all shapes and sizes.

If I can just find... ah, white spirit! How appropriate, thought Leech, as he rushed back into the corridor. He wrenched the lid off the plastic container and sloshed the liquid between himself and the howling ghosts.

"Get back!" he shouted hysterically, whipping a gold-plated lighter from his pocket. "Back or I'll burn you out of existence. I can stay here all night. Help will come in the morning. You daren't walk through fire!"

In unison, the plague-ridden phantoms closed in on Leech. The crazed businessman flicked his lighter and a wall of fire erupted in front of him.

For a moment, Leech stood transfixed by the sheet of flame engulfing his family business. *What had he done?*

He glanced down at the lighter in his hand. It had belonged to his father, who'd given it to him just before he passed away. Suddenly the old man's dying words echoed in his son's head. *Don't make the same mistakes I did, Robert.* But it was too late to change now, surely?

His thoughts were broken by a blotched hand reaching out through the fire.

"The dead may not perish twice, Leech," said the bearded ghost calmly, as he and his fellow ghosts floated through the flames towards him with outstretched arms...

Emerging from the hustle and bustle of a London street, the man in the trilby hat picked up a free newspaper from a stand outside the railway station.

Globe-Aid Centre opened! read the headline.

Yesterday saw the official opening of the new London headquarters of Globe-Aid.

The building is located on the site of the former Leech Investments Building, which had stood since 1670, before it was destroyed by fire 18 months ago.

The cause of the blaze was never discovered. Ex-company director, Robert Leech, who was the only person in the building at the time of the fire, was miraculously found unharmed in the ashes, though with no memory of his previous life. He later donated his entire fortune to Globe-Aid and is now its London representative.

During the demolition of the old building, a 17th century plague pit was discovered under the foundations. The remains of those buried in the pit have since been moved to holy ground.

Globe-Aid is a charitable organization aimed at helping the poorest members of our society.

The man in the trilby hat smiled to himself, folded the newspaper, tucked it under his arm, and disappeared into the crowd.

The Fishermen

"It was a dark and stormy night. On top of the icy black water bobbed a boat, all alone in miles and miles of empty sea."

"Boring!" interrupted a loud voice. "You must have told this one a thousand times, Kristian!"

Ivan wasn't in the mood for another one of Kristian's creepy ghost stories.

True, there wasn't much else to do on board their fishing boat, cooped up for the third week in a row. But there was something about the cramped cabin that spooked him.

"Let him tell the story, Ivan," said the youngest member of their crew. It was Axel's first trip to sea, and he was still enthralled by Kristian's tall tales.

Kristian ignored the interruptions and continued his tale. "It was barely fifty years ago, on this very stretch of water... A fisherman was standing on deck, his oilskin wrapped around him to keep out the driving rain and the biting wind. The boat rocked faster, and any drops of water that splashed onto the deck froze, instantly.

Now, boys, we know that a bad storm can hit fast. But this fisherman had a big reason to worry.

You see, beside him on deck, trembling with cold and fear, was his young wife. She had begged him to take her with him on his first fishing trip after their wedding, just the day before.

The morning had been sunny and clear and the fisherman thought there would be no harm in taking her out on the boat.

But then the sky turned blacker, and they lost sight of the shore.

The fisherman couldn't find his way back and all communication was lost. Fierce waves swept them towards a rocky island.

In the middle of the island, the fisherman could see an old lighthouse, abandoned and completely empty.

He feared for both their lives if they struggled on as they were, so he decided to leave his wife sheltering in the lighthouse while he went to find help."

Kristian paused dramatically, and Axel took the bait. "What happened next? Tell us!" he said eagerly.

Kristian stroked his beard. Solemnly, he continued: "The girl's husband never came back for her. He was lost at sea and his fishing boat was never found. And the girl? Oh, they found her eventually, but by then it was too late. They say that her ghost has haunted the old lighthouse ever since..."

For a moment, his audience was silent. The only noise came from outside, where the wind was rattling the railings on deck.

Ivan scoffed loudly. "Nonsense!" he said. "You really do make up some drivel, Kristian."

The story-teller simply shrugged.

That night, Axel lay awake in his bunk, as Ivan snored nearby. It would be his turn to take over the controls soon, so he should really get some sleep, but the thought of the haunted lighthouse was keeping him wide awake.

"Don't be silly," he told himself. "You're not a kid now. You know perfectly well there are no such things as ghosts."

But there was something about spending week after endless week with only two other people and some wet fish for company to make your mind play crazy tricks on you.

Axel must have fallen asleep, because he was woken by the sound of frantic banging on the cabin door.

"Storm's coming!" Kristian was yelling. "We're taking on water. Everyone on deck!"

Axel hauled himself out of bed and pulled on his boots, stumbling past Ivan who was hurriedly doing the same. They scrambled onto the deck, struggling to keep their balance as a freezing wind rocked the boat almost onto its side.

The three men rushed to bail the water out of the boat, but it was pouring in too fast.

"Throw the fishing nets overboard!" Kristian yelled, but his voice was taken by the wind and didn't reach the other two.

Kristian ran to the control deck and battled to

swing the ship around. They were miles from the safety of the shore, but he could just make out the jagged rocks of an island in the distance. If they could make it there, they could try to anchor the boat to the rocks and find some shelter until the storm passed.

The boat strained against the wind, but Kristian managed to turn it, and they set off towards the rocks. Axel and Ivan had to cling onto the railings just to keep on their feet.

Kristian steered a careful course and, as soon as they were near enough, the fishermen jumped overboard, splashing through the water and dragging the boat with all their strength onto the rocks. Kristian looped a cable around a jutting rock. He hoped that the boat would still be there after the storm passed, but knew it might not be.

In all the confusion, Axel was suddenly still. He had just seen something that swept a new chill over his already frozen body. Stretching up into the churning sky above them was a tall, round building – a lighthouse.

Was it the lighthouse from the story?

As soon as the thought entered his mind, Axel shook it off. They had more than enough real things to worry about, without silly ghost stories.

"This way!" he screamed, over the din of the waves crashing onto the rocks. "We can shelter in the lighthouse!"

The three men scrambled towards it. The sharp rocks cut into their fingers through their gloves, but they were too cold and numb to notice. Once they reached the lighthouse, its heavy wooden door swung open to greet them. It was as if it had opened by itself.

"It's only the wind," Axel told himself.

The door shut behind them again with a bang. Then, silence... The thick walls of the lighthouse completely shut out the noise of the storm.

Axel had never been inside a lighthouse. They had all been closed down years ago, and there certainly weren't any lighthouse keepers around any more. The place was deserted.

"Well, I suppose we stay here until the storm passes," said Ivan. He and Kristian sat down to empty the sea water out of their boots and wring out their soaking socks.

Axel was too shaken up to sit still. He found his way through the gloom to a rickety spiral staircase in the middle of the lighthouse. Gingerly, he started to climb.

At the top of the staircase was the lantern room, where the lighthouse keeper would have fired up the lantern in years past to keep ships from crashing on the rocks. There was nothing here now though, apart from the massive old oil lamp, lit by a shaft of moonlight.

Axel had turned around to go back downstairs, when he thought he heard something. It sounded like the strike of a match, loud in the silence behind him. He must have imagined it. Or perhaps it was the water in his ears.

As he spun back, it was clear he hadn't

imagined anything. Before him, he saw the flickering flame of a match. And, holding the match, partially lit by its orange glow, was a girl. Her skin was as white as fish flesh. She was staring at him, her eyes filled with sadness.

Axel felt as if the water in his boots had just turned to solid ice. He opened his mouth to say something, but his tongue was frozen too. *Who was this girl? The lighthouse keeper? But there weren't any lighthouse keepers!*

Shielding the match, the girl went over to the oil lamp, opened the little door, and lit the wick. The lamp started to glow brighter...

and brighter... until Axel could see the beam spreading out into the black night.

The girl turned to face him again. She opened her mouth, but when she spoke, it sounded as if it was a voice inside Axel's head, not a girl speaking to him from across the room.

"You must never tell anyone you've seen me," the voice said, right inside Axel's brain.

Axel shivered. "I-I promise," he whispered.

The girl moved away from him, standing directly in the bright glare of the lamp. The light was shining into her eyes, but she never blinked. The light shone brighter. To Axel's horror, her eyes disappeared as the light shone right through her skull and out the other side. Then her hands, her hair, her dress...

She seemed to be melting into rays of light.

'To Axel's horror, her eyes disappeared as the light shone right through her skull...'

Axel had to shield his eyes against the fierce glare, and felt his forehead prickle with sweat.

As if snuffed by an invisible hand, the oil lamp flickered and died, plunging the room into darkness. In that instant, Axel knew he was alone. The girl had disappeared.

He ran over to the oil lamp and reached a shaking hand towards it. But even though it had housed a burning flame just moments before, the metal was cold when he touched it, as if there had been no fire at all. In shock and exhaustion, Axel collapsed.

He was woken for a second time by the sound of shouting.

"Hello? Are you up here? Axel?"

Prying open his salty eyelids, he saw two men at the top of the stairs. Rescue had arrived. The men led Axel to a sea ambulance waiting by the rocks below. Already sitting on deck, wrapped in foil blankets, were Kristian and Ivan.

"How did you find us?" Axel asked, once the fishermen had been warmed up with some hot chocolate, and the boat was speeding back to land.

"We saw a light shining from the lighthouse late last night," said one of the rescue men. "That lighthouse has been deserted for a hundred years – we knew it had to be someone in trouble."

Ivan looked at Axel strangely. "You were the one who went up to the lantern room, Axel," he said. "You must have been the one to light the oil lamp."

"Who else could it have been?" agreed Kristian.

Axel remembered the promise he had made to

the girl in the lantern room, and kept quiet.

Could she have been the ghost of the fisherman's young wife, lighting the lamp in the hope of guiding her husband back after all those years? Or was she simply determined no one else should suffer his fate?

Axel shook his head to clear it. He had no way of knowing.

Fishermen don't give up after one bad storm, and Axel kept working on fishing boats for many years. He never forgot what he saw in the lighthouse, but he never told anyone either.

Some years later he married, and his new wife asked him to take her out for a trip on his fishing boat. "Please Axel," she begged. "It's such a beautiful day. It would be fun."

"Not today, my love," he replied, and quickly changed the subject.

She asked a few times more over the years, but he always refused, without ever being able to tell her why...

It was the last day of the winter term. In the little schoolhouse at the edge of the woods, all the slates had been wiped clean and put away inside desks, and there was an air of excitement as the pupils said their goodbyes and set off home for a glorious, school-free week.

The winter sun was already low in the sky, its coppery glow veiled by swirling snow, as the schoolmaster looked out from the door of the schoolhouse across the low, flat landscape. He peered uneasily into the gathering gloom, listening to the howling of the wind.

"Be careful, lads," he warned the last two pupils as they set off. "This snow is bad. It'll be dark soon too, and there's no moon tonight. Best borrow my lantern as you're cutting across country. I'll be right enough on the main road."

The brothers nodded and muttered, shy at this special attention from their teacher. But once he had gone, his feet crunching through the snow as he strode down the main road, they were glad of the lantern. The whirling snowflakes and moaning gusts quickly muffled his retreating form and the sound of his footsteps. As the two boys clambered over the stile and started along the field path, they felt as if they were the only souls stirring out of doors for miles around.

It was a good five miles from the school house to the cottage where the boys lived, tucked away at the far end of the village across the river. In good weather, they could do the walk in less than an hour. But by the time they had crossed the second field, and were shuffling up to their ankles in freezing snow, they knew it was going to take them much longer this evening. The snowflakes were larger and wetter now, and the boys' leather boots were already wet through, the icy damp making their toes curl.

Snow was piled up around the base of the field gate, so it was hard to push open. After much puffing and panting, the boys climbed over it instead, sitting on the top for a moment to catch their breath. As they sat there, the wind gusted around their heads with a shrill wail. Hastily, they jumped down from the gate, but Tom, the

elder brother, let out a wail of his own and almost dropped the lantern.

"It's my ankle, Ted," he gasped, "I think I've twisted it or something."

Ted looked anxiously at his brother. Tom tried standing, and winced from the pain. Then, leaning heavily on the gate, he unwound his muffler and wound it tightly around his ankle.

"There," he said, winking at his little brother, "almost as good as new."

But all the same, he was limping badly as they set off down the path through the woods. The trees gave the boys some shelter from the wind, but snow had piled up all along the path. In places, they were wading knee-deep. Although Tom didn't complain, Ted could tell from the way his mouth was clenched that his ankle was hurting badly.

"Let me take the lantern," he offered, trying to sound braver than he felt. "I'll go first and make a track for you through the deep spots."

"Sometimes, you're not so bad, even for a baby brother," Tom grinned gratefully.

Ted trudged ahead, pushing the snow aside

with his boots as best he could, but it was no good. Tom was hobbling more and more slowly, his face frowning with pain. Before long, he was lagging far behind.

"Ted!" he called, "It's no use. I'm going to have to rest for a while." He sat down on a tree stump and pulled his coat around him, turning up the collar.

"Don't you worry," he said. "It's out of the wind just here, so I'll be snug as anything. You take the lamp and run on home. Ask Father to bring the pony and trap for me."

"All right then..." Ted nodded, hoping his voice sounded normal. He could feel little stabs of fear in his stomach at the thought of having to go on through the dark woods on his own.

"But," he told himself firmly, "it's worse for

Tom, sitting there all alone in the dark."

At least he would have the light.

"I won't be long, I promise," he called as he set off. It was completely dark by now. The lantern cast a bobbing pool of yellow light around Ted's feet, but somehow it only made everything beyond seem blacker and more menacing. He tried hard not to look up at the looming, inky shapes the trees made.

Ted hadn't really liked the path through the woods, ever since he had heard the talk of the boys in the schoolyard a few months back. They had spoken in hushed, excited voices of a vague shape that lurked in the shadows behind the trees, glowing eyes that peered out from the darkness, and strange, ghostly howls that could be heard on stormy nights. Ted had laughed off the stories at the time, but tonight, it felt as though there really might be something dangerous waiting there in the blackness, just behind the veil of whirling snowflakes.

The wind felt less fierce here, but it made a high-pitched, whining noise as it blew through the branches of the trees overhead. Every so often the tone changed and it became a wailing cry, making Ted shudder and quicken his pace. The path seemed narrower tonight, and every few yards black branches, their twiggy fingers twitching in the wind, thrust out at him, catching on his coat sleeve.

Once, he nearly dropped the lantern. His hand trembled as tried to shake off the feeling that something in the woods was trying to stop him, to put out the light.

Ted was beginning to feel he had been trudging through the woods forever when the turn-off to the little bridge loomed into view. Here the trees thinned out slightly and the path wound alongside the river. Ted hurried forward, his heart thumping with relief to be leaving the thick shadows of the trees.

Out of the woods he felt safe again, but the wind was twice as strong, and Ted staggered whenever a blast caught him. All he could see of the water was a faint, dark gleam, but its swollen, rushing sound filled his ears and made his head swim.

"Just around this corner, then over the bridge, and I'm almost there," Ted muttered, quickening his pace still more. Half-running, half-stumbling through the snow, he came to the spot where the bridge, a rough platform nailed together from planks, left the path. Beyond it, screened from view by a short wooded path, were the first few houses of the village and, beyond them, home.

Ted hurried forward, but at the foot of the bridge, something made him pause. He held up the lantern and could just make out the first few steps of the way across. The planks were covered with snow – not deeply, but enough to make them slippery underfoot. The wind seemed even fiercer now, its chilling howls blending with the gurgling shout of the river. The bridge shuddered. Ted felt a prickle of fear.

What if he slipped and slid off the bridge into the icy water? In the dark, and with the river running high, he wouldn't have a chance. Even if someone did hear his cries above the noise of wind and water, he would be swept away before anyone could come to help.

The planks gave another shuddering groan. Fighting a rising feeling of panic in his chest, he tried to think clearly. He was so nearly home, it seemed silly not to risk a dash across the bridge. There was another way – around by the main road bridge – but that would take him another half an hour at least. And all that time, Tom would be left freezing in the woods.

Ted made up his mind. Whatever the risk, he had to get home as quickly as he could. He would take his chance on the slippery planks.

But just as he went to step forward onto the bridge, he froze.

Beyond the circle of lamplight, from the middle of the bridge, two round, bright spots of light shone out. Ted felt his heart thumping madly in his chest and the hairs on the back of his neck stood up, as he realized they were eyes. Two enormous eyes, with a vivid green glow, staring right at him.

All the stories he had heard in the schoolyard rushed back to Ted's mind and he let out a yelp, but somehow he couldn't lift his feet or look away. He simply stood there, rigid with horror, as the eyes came closer, until they were at the very edge of the circle of lamplight. Ted braced himself, expecting – he didn't know what… A snarl, a flash of claws, a swift and deadly bite?

'Two enormous eyes, with a vivid green glow, staring right at him.'

And then a small, white cat stepped daintily into the light. It looked up at Ted, its green eyes shining, and put out a delicate paw to touch the toe of his boot, in a friendly, questioning way.

Ted laughed out loud in relief.

"It's only a cat!" he choked, struggling to control his breath. "What are you doing out here on a night like this, kitty?"

Ted bent down to stroke the cat. Its soft, white fur felt warm and dry, despite the snow flurries eddying around it. He could feel it purring, as it rubbed itself gently around his legs.

"Well," said Ted, feeling much better, "nice to meet you, kitty, but I have to get on."

He straightened up and moved forward again. At once, the cat stopped purring and backed towards the bridge, staring up at him.

"Shoo!" called Ted. "Out of the way!"

But the cat wouldn't move. It arched its back and stuck its tail straight up in the air, its eyes glowing bright green again.

Ted took another step forward. At this, the cat started hissing fiercely, its fur standing on end. Ted was sure he could see tiny sparks flying from its body – or was it was a trick of the lamplight and the falling snow?

He had a feeling that, for some reason, the cat didn't want him to cross the bridge, but that was silly. It was the quickest way home, and the quickest way

of getting help for Tom. He had to go across – and the sooner, the better.

Just then, the wind gave a particularly vicious wail and the snow seemed worse than ever, filling Ted's ears and eyes with clinging, wet flakes. The bridge gave a terrible, creaking sigh. The cat came closer, still arched and hissing.

Ted took a step back, despite himself. He was beginning to wonder if it was such a good idea to risk the plank bridge. Immediately, the cat relaxed and became a small, polite creature once more. It wound around Ted's legs one more time, and then set off along the river bank, stopping after a few paces and looking back at Ted over its shoulder.

"Crazy cat!" Ted muttered to himself, hoping he was doing the right thing. He set off after it, going at a shuffling run as he headed for the main road and the big bridge as fast as he could manage. To his amazement, the cat trotted along a little ahead of him, keeping inside the circle of lamplight, so he could see it clearly.

They won't believe me when I get home, Ted thought. The wind was howling fiercely, and the snow flew past him just as quickly, but the way was clearer here, and somehow Ted felt warmer and happier, despite the longer path he was taking.

He had been going for twenty minutes when he glimpsed the lights of a low-roofed cottage by the turning to the road bridge. As the cat passed the gate it looked back at him, gave a small meow, turned and ran quickly up the garden path.

That must be where it lives, thought Ted.

And then, *Uh-oh.*

Several pale circles of light were bobbing up and down in the darkness beyond the trees. They seemed to float above the ground, and they were moving towards him fast.

Ted gulped, feeling very much alone without the cat trotting ahead. Panicked, he turned to run.

At that moment, he heard a familiar voice.

"Ted, is that you?" it cried, and Ted saw his father stride out of the gloom, surrounded by men with lanterns. "Where's Tom?" his father asked immediately, but hurried on, "Thank goodness you had the sense to come the long way home. The news is all over the village. The plank bridge gave way a few minutes ago. Old Mr. Reeve saw it go. He was trying to get across from our side. It couldn't stand all this wind and the high river."

Ted looked at him and gulped.

"That cat!" he mumbled, amazed. "I knew it didn't want me to cross! It must have known..."

"Cat?" echoed his father, "What on earth?"

"You must go and get Tom right away!" said Ted hurriedly, explaining where he had left him. His father left quickly to collect the pony and trap, leaving Ted stumbling along behind him, on his own once more, his mind buzzing with unanswered questions.

It was only the next day, when Tom was safely home, sitting by the fire with his ankle swathed in bandages, that Ted decided to visit the cottage by the bridge for news of the white cat.

"Come in," beamed the old lady who lived there. "Let me get you a cocoa."

Bustling in her kitchen, she went on. "Yes, I had a white cat. Must have been forty years ago, now. Pretty little thing she was. I called her Snowy. Though that was unfortunate, considering... She was out one night – always liked to go mousing in the woods – when a terrible snowstorm blew up. Rather like the one last night, come to think of it. I never saw her again, poor thing. She must have lost her way and perished from the cold."

"Do you know," the old lady continued thoughtfully, "the strange thing is that, on snowy nights, I sometimes think I can hear that cat meowing outside my house. But when I open the front door, there's nothing there."

The Haunted Hill

Hundreds of years ago in the Japanese region of Edo, a merchant was hurrying home after a day at work. His name was Kunimura, and he was rather pleased with himself. "I can't believe I managed to seal the deal!" he exclaimed, chuckling with glee.

Kunimura had just sold his entire stock of expensive silk to a young lord.

It had taken all day and most of the evening to come to an agreement, but, at last, Kunimura had walked away a rich man. He patted his robes, feeling the heavy pouch of coins hidden inside them, and grinned a satisfied grin.

So far, Kunimura's journey home had been uneventful. His dealings with the lord had gone on for so long that the roads were deserted. The sky was as black as ink, and the only light came from a pale moon and the fragile paper lantern he held in one hand.

As Kunimura was making his way along the Akasaka Road, still congratulating himself on his bartering skills, he noticed another lantern glowing ahead of him. Peering into the gloom, he saw a shadowy figure coming his way.

All at once, Kunimura felt vulnerable. He was

carrying a lot of money, and the last thing he wanted was to be robbed. Carefully, he pulled his robes tightly around his body, set his mouth in a firm line and walked on, a little more nervously than before.

When at last their paths crossed, Kunimura let out a small sigh. It was only a noodle seller.

"Good evening," said the man, with a bow, smiling warmly.

"And to you," replied Kunimura, bowing in turn. He was about to continue on his way, when the noodle seller stopped him in his stride.

"I wouldn't go down that road if I were you," said the noodle seller.

"What? Why not?" asked Kunimura.

Instantly, his mind jumped to visions of bandits lurking in the shadows. He had to stop himself from reaching for his coin pouch.

"Don't you know?" said the man, his eyes darting around nervously. "It leads to Kinokuni Hill. Surely you must have heard of the haunted hill. Aren't you afraid of ghosts?"

Kunimura laughed out loud. He couldn't help himself. He knew all about the so-called 'haunted hill'. It was once home to a great lord, who had lived there in a grand castle surrounded by a moat. Eventually the lord had passed away, and the castle was destroyed. Ever since then, people who walked up the hill at night claimed they heard odd whisperings and saw strange things moving around in the dark.

"Oh, you had me worried there," said Kunimura, in between chuckles. "You had me thinking there were *real* dangers up ahead. Bandits perhaps, or wild animals. But *ghosts?* Who's afraid of ghosts?"

"Don't say I didn't warn you," said the noodle seller, shaking his head. He raised his lantern, turned and walked away.

Kunimura hurried faster now, determined to get home so that he could lock his money safely away, then settle down to a well-deserved supper.

When he arrived at the foot of Kinokuni Hill, he paused. *What if there were some truth to the noodle seller's words?* Then again, if he changed his route now, it would take hours to get home.

"No," he said, decisively, tightening his grip on his lantern. "I won't change my mind just because of a few silly stories." He reached for his coin pouch. Feeling it there, safe and sound, he remembered his earlier joy at his success. And, with a grin on his face once more, he started up the hill.

Kunimura wasn't even halfway up when he heard sobbing. It was quiet at first, barely recognizable over the sound of the chirping cicadas. But soon it became more and more insistent. Kunimura looked around for whoever – or whatever – was making the noise. The grin on his face faded, and his mind filled once again with all the horrors that might await him.

Instead, he found a girl. She was sitting away from the road, dressed in beautiful scarlet robes embroidered with firebirds in flight. Her face was buried in her voluminous sleeves and she was weeping so fiercely that her entire body shook.

"What are you doing out here?" asked Kunimura, his voice loud with shock. Instead of replying, the girl continued to weep.

"I'm sorry," he said, more quietly. "I hope I didn't frighten you."

He took a step forwards and realized that the girl was almost at the edge of a dried-up river, shrouded in darkness. No, not a river – the moat. It was all that was left of the castle on Kinokuni Hill.

The merchant studied the girl. Her hair was unbound and bedraggled, falling to her waist. Her sleeves were soaked through with tears. She was so very sad. What on earth could be wrong?

"Don't worry," said Kunimura, taking another step towards her, "I won't hurt you. Please, don't cry. Tell me, what's the matter? I'll help you, if I possibly can."

But still the girl didn't reply. She simply buried her face deeper into her sleeves and bawled even harder than before.

"Come now, it can't be that bad, can it?" Kunimura said, after a while. He risked another step closer, not knowing how she might react. "You're in good company here. I'll keep you safe. Just please, stop crying."

As he said this, he raised his lantern in front of him so he could see her more clearly.

That was when the girl stopped weeping. Slowly, very slowly, she pulled her sleeves away from her face, then turned to meet Kunimura, whose eyes grew wide with fear. Because what Kunimura saw when he looked at the girl's face was... nothing. Instead of eyes, a nose and a mouth, the girl's face was completely smooth, like the surface of an egg.

Kunimura screamed. In a moment of pure terror, he threw his lantern at the girl and fled, running up Kinokuni Hill as fast as he could. He glanced back only once, and saw that same blank face illuminated in the dark.

He ran on and on, his heart hammering in his chest, until he reached the top of the hill. His legs gave way, and he slumped to the ground at the side of the road, unable to go any further. His entire body was drenched in sweat, and his mind was racing. He looked behind him, petrified by what he might see, and saw nothing but blackness.

"What was that thing?" he asked himself, clutching his chest as he gasped for breaths. "Some kind of monster? A ghost?"

Then he felt it. Or rather, *didn't* feel it. "Where is it?" he cried, jumping to his feet and patting himself all over. "My money – it's gone!"

From out of the blackness, Kunimura heard a girlish giggle. His eyes darted around, but he couldn't make out a thing in the dark.

Suddenly, a light started glowing in a nearby tree. Kunimura looked up and there, stuck in the highest branch, was his lantern. And hanging

from its handle was…

"My coin pouch!" Kunimura cried. *How was this possible? Had the ghost left it there? What kind of crazy trick was this?*

Kunimura waited a moment, keeping an eye out for anything suspicious. But when nothing else happened, he decided to risk rescuing it.

He kicked off his sandals, slipped off his outer robes, then used a strap of cloth to tie back his long sleeves. When he was ready, he approached the tree and, branch by branch, began to climb.

It wasn't easy. At one point his robe snagged when he was reaching for his next handhold and he slipped. Luckily he managed to catch the branch below, just in time to save himself from a nasty fall. As it was, he tore a huge hole in his best outfit.

Finally, Kunimura made it to the highest branch. He hugged it to his chest, then, very carefully, crawled out along it. The lantern and the coin pouch were almost within his grasp when, down below, he heard the same girlish giggle as before.

Looking to the ground, Kunimura saw the ghost from the hill, her flaming red robes and blank face standing out as if it were day.

Without a word, she reached down and picked up his sandals and robes, then slipped them into her sleeves.

"What do you think you're doing?" Kunimura shouted. "Put those back!"

Instead, the girl pointed up, past him to where the lantern and his coin pouch were hanging. Kunimura turned to look at them,

'The lantern and the coin pouch were almost within his grasp...'

only to discover that they had vanished.

In a surge of anger, Kunimura whipped his head around and glared at the girl. There she stood, his lantern in one hand and his coin pouch in the other. Had she a face, Kunimura would have sworn she was grinning at him.

Kunimura howled and screamed. He looked for something to throw at the ghost, but there was nothing close by. He tried to shuffle back to the trunk, so he could climb down, but it was too late. The girl was already walking away, fading with every step she took. When she reached the road, she simply disappeared as if she had been nothing more than a daydream, taking his lantern, his pouch and his sandals with her.

Kunimura stayed motionless in the tree for a long time, unable to accept what had just

happened. Finally, he started to make his way back down.

Coming down was a lot more difficult than going up had been, especially in the dark. When at last he reached the ground, his robes were in tatters, and his arms and legs were covered in scratches and scrapes.

"How did this happen?" he asked himself. "Where did I go wrong?"

In the space of a single evening, Kunimura had gained enough money to buy a small house, then lost it all to something that – until tonight – he hadn't even believed existed.

With a heavy heart, Kunimura returned to the road and started to stagger home. At one point, he stepped on a particularly sharp stone and yelped.

"If only I had listened to the noodle seller," he sulked aloud. "If only I hadn't been so foolish and gone up that haunted hill. Now look at me – my money gone, my clothes nothing but rags, and my feet covered in cuts and blisters."

"But at least you still have your life," came a friendly voice from in front of him.

Kunimura looked up and there, coming towards him, was the noodle seller, smiling as warmly as ever, a lantern swinging in his hand.

"Come," he said, calmly. "My stall is just down the road. It's not open yet, but you look as if you could do with a good meal."

A little while later, Kunimura was wolfing down a meal of hot soba noodles, pausing every now and then to tell the noodle seller all about his misfortunes.

"...and when she looked at me, she had no face – none at all."

"Ah, so you saw a headless ghost?" said the noodle seller, thoughtfully.

"No, no," said Kunimura, slurping down the last of his noodles. "She had a head, but her face was blank. She had no eyes, no nose, no mouth – nothing."

"I see," said the noodle seller, taking away Kunimura's empty bowl.

At once, Kunimura felt guilty, first for ignoring the noodle seller's warnings, and then for taking his food, too. "I'm sorry," he said. "I would pay you if I could, but the ghost took my money."

"Oh really?" chuckled the noodle seller. "Well, perhaps I can help you out. I recently came across a small fortune. I'd be happy to lend you some money for your journey home." And with that, he pulled out a heavy coin pouch from inside his robe – a very familiar coin pouch – and started rummaging inside.

"Where... where did you get that?" said Kunimura, with a tremor in his voice.

Rather than answer, the noodle seller lowered the pouch to the table with a *clink*, then replied with a question of his own.

"Tell me," he asked, "did your ghost look something like this...?"

The noodle seller stroked his face, and at once his features disappeared.

It was as if his eyes, nose and mouth had all been painted on, only to be wiped away by that simple gesture.

Kunimura leaped to his feet just as the lights went out, plunging him into darkness. And all around him came a girlish giggle, echoing through the night...

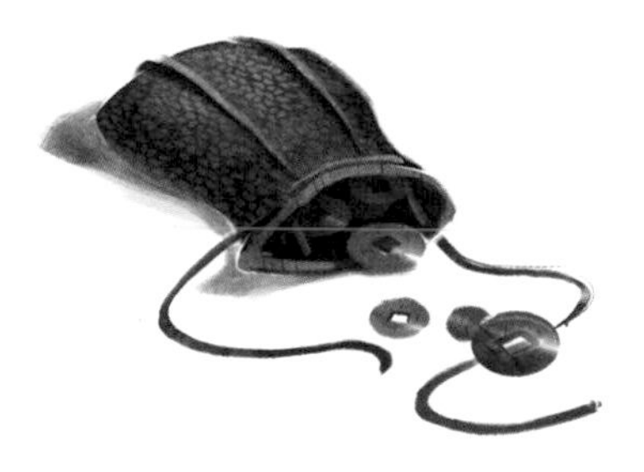

Mr. Coombes

Scarsbrook was one of the most prestigious schools in the country. With its imposing red-brick boarding houses, vast playing fields and pupils dressed in tailcoats and bow ties, it looked nothing like my old school. I'd spent my first day feeling overwhelmed and lost, and was relieved I'd made it to the last lesson without trouble.

"Pssst! Charlie!" came a whisper from behind me. "Can I borrow a pencil sharpener?"

Oh Harry, why now? I thought. It was nearly the end of the lesson and we weren't meant to make a sound in class.

"Pssst!" he hissed again, insistently.

I waited until Mr. McNeil turned to write on the board, carefully picked up my pencil sharpener, and reached back to pass it to Harry. I felt his sticky hand take hold of it and then…

RATaTACKaTACK! It fell with a clatter onto the hard wooden floor. Mr. McNeil swung around, glared at the sharpener, and bellowed, "Whose is that?!"

"M… mine, sir," I said, and felt my face flushing red.

"I was just about to borrow it because I'd

forgotten my–" Harry butted in, but he didn't get the chance to finish.

"Quiet, Burgess!" snapped the teacher. "As for you, *new boy*, take this!" He tore a pink slip from a book, scribbled a few words, and passed it to me. "That's for tonight, after school, in the library."

My heart sank. Detention. It wasn't the best way to finish my first day. At that very moment, the bell rang for the end of school.

"Run along then," Mr. McNeil said. "The headmistress will be waiting."

I packed up my things as Harry gave me an apologetic look, and trooped off down the corridor, into the biting wind outside.

As I tried to remember the way through the cloisters to the library, I cursed my luck. *What a way to start at my new school...*

When I reached the grand stone archway at the entrance to the library, Mrs. Thackray, the haggard old headmistress, was indeed waiting. "Just the one of you this evening, is it?" she barked and took my slip. "A new one too. Talking in class hmm? Well, you'll be quiet in here. Get in and sit down," she added, pointing to a table in the corner.

The library was hundreds of years old, and the only building to have survived a fire that destroyed the rest of the school many years before. It was cold and cavernous, with bookshelves on all sides. Black iron chandeliers holding glowing candles hung from the ceiling and dusty cobwebs were laced across every nook and cranny. Even when it was full of people studying on a warm summer's day it wouldn't exactly be inviting, but now it was dark and empty, with a winter chill in the air.

Mrs. Thackray glanced around, shivered at a gust of wind, and promptly decided: "I have better things to do than sit in here with you."

She reached up and pulled a thick cloth-bound book off the shelf.

"Here, copy that out," she said, dropping it onto the table with a thud. A cloud of dust rose from the cover, revealing its title: 'The History of Scarsbrook School for Boys'.

"No point in wasting your time," said the headmistress. "You may as well learn something while you sit here."

With that, she pulled open the library door and strode back to her office.

The book looked as if it hadn't been read for years. I turned to the contents page and scanned the chapter titles.

Chapter 1: Departments

Chapter 2: Facilities

Chapter 3: Rules and regulations

And then, further down the page, a chapter caught my eye…

Chapter 13: Mr. Coombes, the hero of Scarsbrook

I wasn't sure if I was meant to simply start copying from page 1, but the headmistress hadn't

specifically said to and this chapter sounded interesting, so I flicked through the pages to find it.

Just then, I heard a scuffling sound behind the bookshelves on the far side of the library.

And then…

Creeeeeak.

What was that? I thought with a start, looking up nervously. I couldn't see anything. "It's an old building," I told myself. "Of course it creaks."

Feeling a little foolish, and glad that no one had been around to see me, I turned back to the book, and began to copy it out.

> There was barely anything out of the ordinary about the teacher, Mr. Stanley Coombes. In appearance, he could hardly have been a more typical man of the time.

He doesn't sound much like a hero yet, I thought, intrigued, as I read on.

> His black robes hung loosely on his slender frame, which rose to a very average 5 feet and 10 inches, and his soft brown hair parted neatly across his head. Perhaps his one distinctive feature was a pair of steel-rimmed spectacles, which were noticeably scratched after years of wear and tear.

Suddenly I heard the sound of footsteps from behind the bookcases nearest to me.

Clack… clack… clack…

This time, I jumped in my seat. There *was* someone else in here.

"Hello?" I called out. There was no reply.

Strange… I thought, shifting uncomfortably.

I tried to reassure myself. Maybe there was a

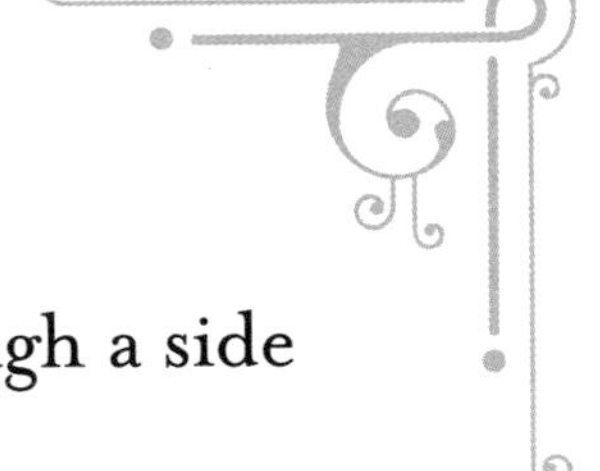

caretaker and he'd let himself in through a side door I hadn't noticed.

But then why didn't I hear a door?

Or maybe... maybe some other boys were playing tricks on me, 'the new boy'. Yes, that was probably it. I shook myself out of my panic. If I didn't focus, I would be in even more trouble with Mrs. Thackray. Back to the book...

> Mr. Coombes was a fresh-faced, intelligent young teacher of English, with a special interest in medieval folktales, which he dearly loved studying in the library. He was respected by colleagues and well-liked by his pupils, who admired his kind heart, willingness to listen, and wise words of advice.

Clack... clack... went the footsteps again.

Who was it?

'With my heart pumping in my chest, I looked around the end of the bookcase.'

Silently, I left my chair and crept across the waxy wooden floor between two bookcases.

In the flickering candlelight I could just about see through gaps in the rows of books. As I peered into the gloom, something glided by. Something that was definitely not a caretaker, or a pupil. No, this was a shadowy figure dressed in a long, loose, dark robe.

"Hello?" I tried again.

Silence. But there, where I'd just seen the mysterious figure, one of the books started to slide slowly off the shelf.

"Whoever you are, please come out," I said, hoping that my voice didn't sound as frightened as I felt.

Still no reply. *Come on Charlie, be brave.*

With my heart pumping in my chest, I looked

around the end of the bookcase.

Standing in front of me was a young teacher I hadn't seen before. He had a friendly air about him, with floppy dark brown hair and scratched, steel-rimmed glasses.

"You know, you ought not to talk in a library, young man," he said. "But I won't tell if you won't," he added. "Now, I'd like to catch up on some reading." He held up his book: 'Arthurian Legends'. "And I suppose you'd better be getting on with your work, before the headmistress comes back."

"O… oh… ok," I stuttered.

"By the way, I believe it gets a good deal more interesting over the page," he said, smiling kindly.

How does he know what I'm reading?

Confused, I went back to my table, turned the

page and read on. The teacher was right. It got a lot more exciting.

With parts of the school now ablaze, Mr. Coombes hurried to make sure the pupils were evacuated safely.

When it emerged that a boy named Peter Baglow was still inside, he charged back in to rescue him. He found the boy in the library, which was beginning to catch fire.

Peter later told how they climbed a bookcase together, and that Mr. Coombes had hoisted him through an open upper window, from where he could escape across the roof. Tragically, Mr. Coombes was not able to fit through the window himself.

Remarkably, it seems that, knowing his own fate, he set about preserving the library that was so dear to him.

Fire fighters entering the library a short while later found all the books stacked up at the far side of the room, away from the flames which were leaping through the doorway.

Although they arrived in time to save the books, sadly, the heroic schoolmaster had already succumbed to the deadly fog of smoke.

"Wow… what a hero," I said.

"Well, I was only doing my duty. Any decent fellow would do the same," said the teacher, who was now sitting at a table facing me at the far end of the room.

What does he mean 'I'?

"Oh come on dear boy, don't look so bemused. What greater deed can one aspire to than saving another person's life? The books were just a little extra, something to keep me amused on days like today."

But... how? I wondered, as the truth dawned upon me. *He can't be... but he must be... Mr. Coombes!*

At that moment, the library door flew open with a bang.

"What," Mrs. Thackray boomed, her eyes fixed on me as she burst into the room, "is all this racket? I'd have thought your talkative tendencies had got you into enough trouble for one day."

"I... I... there's a g..." I started, my voice trembling as I spoke.

Mr. Coombes, I could see over her shoulder,

was looking sympathetically in my direction. He rose to his feet and began walking towards us.

"Let me see your work," the headmistress demanded, as if I hadn't spoken, She picked up the book and scanned my piece of paper. "Four lines?! Is that all you've managed? Four measly lines? You didn't even start at the beginning!"

"I… I can explain. Or even, maybe, it would be better if… he explained?" I offered, pointing over Mrs. Thackray's shoulder.

"WHO?" bellowed Mrs. Thackray, thumping the book closed and wheeling around.

"Mr. Coo…" I began. "He's gone!"

He must have disappeared when she closed the book.

"Listen here, Cresswell. If you think it's funny to do nothing for an entire detention, and then to try to fool me with tales of some imaginary friend of yours, I can assure you of one thing: you won't be laughing for long."

"But Mrs. Thackray, I promise..."

"Say one more word, boy, just ONE MORE WORD, and you'll be in detention every single day for a year! I swear you won't rest until you have copied out every last word of that book."

I paused for a second. It would be fun to talk to Mr. Coombes again. He could tell me all kinds of things about the school. I wouldn't feel so new and so lost.

I looked up at Mrs. Thackray warily and then said: "Okay."

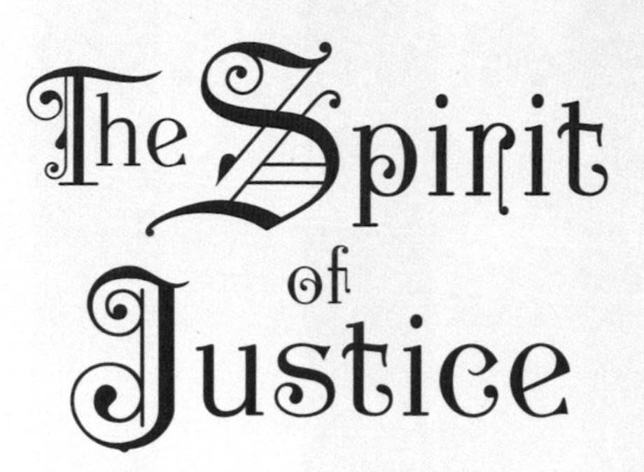

The Spirit of Justice

Verity Whitlock woke with a start. Her skin felt ice-cold.

From the corner of her eye, she saw a blurred white shape dart past her bedroom window, then disappear into the darkness. *What was it?*

For a few moments she stayed completely still, too scared to move.

Ever since she was little, she had heard stories about the house being haunted. Only last week, one of the maids claimed to have seen a ghostly figure in the attic. And the stable boys were always telling tales of a glowing apparition that appeared after dark.

Steeling herself, and with her heart pounding, Verity pushed off her blankets and went to the window. She looked outside for signs of life, noticing the nearby treetops lit up in the moonlight. A movement on the lawn below made her look down, to where the slight figure of a girl was staring at her. Verity guessed that she was about eighteen, the same age as herself.

The girl was dressed completely in white, with skin so pale it almost blended into her clothes. Her dress was old-fashioned, with a tight waist,

a full skirt and long, thin sleeves.

Verity was intrigued. Could this have been the shape at her window? But why was a girl who looked as if she belonged to the 1700s standing in the gardens of Wildebourne Manor on a summer's night in 1835?

Her curiosity overcame her fear. As quietly as she could, Verity pulled on her dressing gown and slippers, crept downstairs and went outside.

At first, the girl seemed to have disappeared but, rounding the corner of the house, Verity saw her again. She was standing between the long row of box hedges that led from the manor house to the river. Seeing the girl close up, Verity gasped. The girl's whole body was fringed by an unearthly shimmering glow, almost as if she were lit from within.

The girl smiled encouragingly, turned and seemed to glide over the grass in the direction of the river.

Verity tried to call out but her mouth was dry. Filled with excitement mixed with fear, she followed the girl down to the riverbank.

"Who are you?" wondered Verity. Something about the girl's delicate features sparked a vague memory.

The girl stretched out an arm and pointed across the river.

Verity peered into the darkness. Somehow she expected to see something as unusual as the girl herself. But the scene was the same as ever. She could hear the River Wilde rushing past, and just make out Traitor's Bridge, the wooden crossing that led to a farm on the other side.

Verity looked back to where the girl had been standing, only to find empty air. The girl had vanished.

After waiting for a minute in case the girl returned, Verity slowly walked back to the house. But she couldn't get to sleep. Her head was filled with too many questions. Who was the unearthly girl? Where had she come from? Where had she gone? And what had she been trying to tell her?

Verity was still puzzling over the night's events when she went down to breakfast.

At the foot of the stairs, she stopped.

There before her was the girl.

Not the ethereal figure of the night before, but a painting, surrounded by many other portraits of the Whitlock family through the ages. Her face looked happier, and her clothes were different, but it was unmistakably the same girl. No wonder she had seemed familiar.

Verity read the inscription on the frame...

...and clutched the bannister in shock, as the full meaning of the dates hit her.

The ice-cold chill had returned to her skin and she shivered. The young girl she'd seen last night had been dead for over eighty years.

The poor thing was only eighteen when she died, thought Verity. *Was she ill? What happened to her?*

She tried asking her parents over breakfast, but neither of them wanted to discuss it.

"That's all in the past," her father said firmly, shaking out his newspaper. "Nothing for you to worry about."

"Listen to your father, dear," added her mother.

So, as soon as she could, Verity left the table and rushed up to her grandmother's room.

The old lady was sitting up in bed, taking her breakfast on a tray as usual.

"A fine hour for such questions," she said in surprise, when Verity asked about Elizabeth.

"I'm sorry, Grandmama," Verity replied, "but I just had to know."

Sensing the urgency in Verity's voice, her grandmother became more sympathetic. She looked at her for a moment, then carefully replaced her teacup on the tray.

"Elizabeth, or Lizzy as I believe she was known by the family, was your great-great-aunt on your father's side. She was a wayward, free-spirited young thing without a care in the world..."

"You knew her?" interrupted Verity.

"Only what I heard," continued Lady Whitlock, with a slight frown at her granddaughter for the interruption. "She died long before I married your grandfather. Apparently she was always out riding in the fields on her own, without even a chaperone.

No one ever knew where she was. I heard that she drove your great-great-grandfather Hugo to distraction. In any case, things came to a head when she started seeing the Mortimer boy..."

"Not the Mortimers of Mill Farm, across the river?" asked Verity.

"The very same," replied her grandmother with a nod. "Needless to say, the match was not considered suitable by her parents. Not that that made any difference to Lizzy.

One afternoon, she and her father had a dreadful argument about the whole business. She wanted to go across the river to see her sweetheart. Her father flatly refused and confined her to the house. But somehow, later that evening, she managed to slip out.

The next morning she was nowhere to be

found. Servants were sent to Mill Farm and the village to ask about her, but no one had seen Lizzy since the previous afternoon."

Verity's grandmother paused, and a grave look crossed her face.

"The following day, Lizzy Whitlock's body was found half a mile down the River Wilde, caught in some tree roots by the riverbank."

Verity shuddered with horror.

"Of course there was an investigation," Lady Whitlock went on. "In fact young Ben Mortimer was arrested on suspicion of murder. Nothing was ever proved, but the boy was cast out from village life from then on.

Naturally the whole Whitlock family was distraught. They say Lizzy's father, Hugo, died of a broken heart shortly afterwards. And your

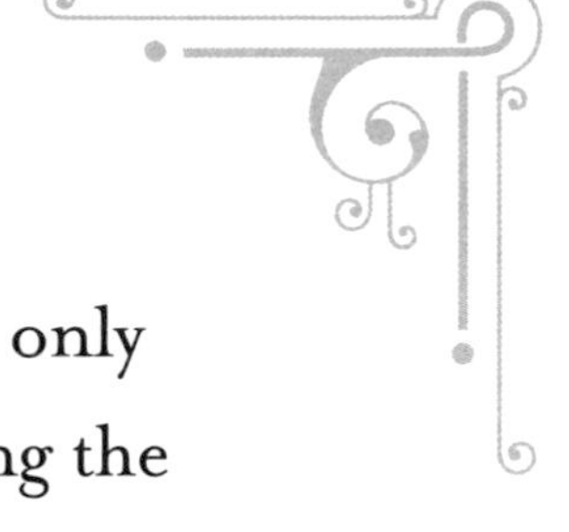

grandfather would never speak of it. I only learned what I've told you from hearing the servants talk."

"What made you so interested in Lizzy?" asked Verity.

Her grandmother looked away. "I think that's quite enough melodrama before breakfast," she replied, and shooed her out.

Verity went out into the grounds to think.

Maybe that's why Lizzy led me to the river?

But she couldn't help feeling there must be more to it. Lizzy had been trying to tell her something. *But what?* Verity recalled the image of the young girl pointing across the river. Perhaps the answer lay at Mill Farm.

She went down to the river, ran lightly across Traitor's Bridge and began to follow the path along the riverbank to the farmhouse.

A middle-aged man opened the door to her hesitant knock.

"Mr. Mortimer?" asked Verity.

"Yes?" he said, giving her a curious look.

"How do you do? I'm Verity Whitlock," she announced. "I'm looking into my family history and I wondered if you knew anything about Lizzy Whitlock and Ben Mortimer?"

"What do you want to go digging that up for, miss?" said Mr. Mortimer curtly.

Verity flushed. "I'm sorry..." she began.

Before she could finish, a hoarse voice called out. "Leave the girl be, lad. You come along inside, miss."

Mr. Mortimer shrugged and stepped aside, gesturing her into a large farmhouse kitchen.

Verity gave him a nervous smile and went in.

Seated in a wooden chair by the window was an old man. His white hair was so fine it was almost transparent, and his skin was bronzed and wrinkled like wizened fruit. But he had a kindly face that instantly made Verity feel at ease.

"So you want to know about young Lizzy?" he asked.

"Yes sir," said Verity. "If you don't mind."

The old man closed his eyes. "Not a day goes by when I don't think of my dear girl," he murmured.

With a start, Verity realized she was talking to Ben Mortimer. *He must be at least a hundred years old.*

In a shaking voice, he told her how he and Lizzy had met when he'd been working in the fields. From that day they had seen each other whenever they could and slowly fell in love.

Verity almost didn't want to ask her next question. But she had to.

"What happened on the night Lizzy...?" She found it impossible to finish the sentence.

Ben sighed. "I wish I knew, lass. If there'd been anything in my power to change things, I would have done it." He paused.

"We were due to meet that afternoon. We'd planned to tell my dad we wanted to wed, you see. We hoped he might persuade Lizzy's father to look kindly on the match, father to father."

Verity realized why Lizzy had been so desperate to get out of the house.

"But she never came?" she asked.

The old man shook his head. "They found her horse, Lightfoot, wandering up by the manor house stables the next morning. Seems Lizzy must have got as far as the river. But whether she ever crossed Traitor's Bridge..."

Verity could see tears welling up in Ben's eyes, so she tried to think of something else, to distract him for a moment.

"Why *do* they call it that?" she asked quickly. "I've often wondered."

"You of all folk ought to know," said Ben with a sniff, seemingly equally glad to change the subject. "It was built by Lizzy's father when she was only a child.

He had a fierce temper did Sir Hugo Whitlock. He'd go into such rages with his servants, they reckoned him half crazy... Oh, I beg your pardon, miss."

Verity smiled to show she wasn't offended.

"Anyway, a few times when servants crossed him, or spoke out against his cruel ways, he'd stuff what little they owned into a couple of canvas sacks. Then he tied the bags to their back, put the poor devils onto an old horse and marched them around the grounds for all to see.

Come nightfall, he led them down to Traitor's Bridge and ordered them across, never to set foot on his land again. No one ever saw this last bit of the performance, mind. He always insisted on seeing 'em off alone."

"What a very strange ritual," said Verity.

Ben nodded. "It worked, though. No one ever came back. Though a couple of the horses did, strangely enough.

Come to think of it, Sir Hugo had seen off his groom the night before Lizzy went missing. Kendrick his name was. He'd complained that a horse was being mistreated and challenged Sir Hugo. They tried tracking Kendrick down in case he'd had anything to do with Lizzy's death, but they never found him."

For a moment, Verity considered asking Ben about his arrest, but thought better of it. She was convinced that he had nothing to do with what happened.

As she walked back along the riverbank, Verity went over what she'd learned.

It seemed clear to her that Lizzy had been late

for her meeting with Ben, so had ridden as far as Traitor's Bridge. *Then what?* If Lightfoot had thrown her by the bank, the water there would have been too shallow for her to drown. So if she fell from her horse, it must have occurred on the bridge. And then Lightfoot had somehow found his way back to the stables?

Verity sighed. She had a lot of questions but very few answers.

She went to bed that night with her mind still in turmoil, and lay awake until past midnight, hoping for another visit from Lizzy's ghost. But by one o'clock, her eyes had begun to close...

She was awoken by a bright, white light, flooding under her door. The icy sensation crept over her skin again. Her heart racing, she went over to the door and tugged it open.

At first, the corridor seemed empty. Then she noticed a white blur, as something darted around the corner at the far end.

Nervously, Verity followed. Part of her wanted to race back to her room, lock the door and hide under her bedcovers. But she ignored that. The braver part of her wanted to solve the mystery.

Turning the corner, she reached the staircase that led up to the attic. The door at the top was slightly ajar. Recalling the terrified housemaid from the week before, Verity wondered if the maid had seen Lizzy. When she pushed the door, it swung open with a nerve-chilling creak.

Verity entered cautiously. She wanted to see Lizzy, but the attic was a dark, eerie place at the best of times. Just now, with strange shadows on the walls, it seemed more frightening than ever.

The room was crammed with old furniture and towers of trunks and boxes containing the unwanted possessions of Verity's ancestors.

Brushing a cobweb from her face, she realized that the shadows were made by a white light, glowing behind a battered chest of drawers. Verity felt the dusty floorboards beneath her bare feet as she tiptoed closer.

Despite half expecting it, Verity jumped as the ghost of Lizzy Whitlock stepped out.

She looked just as she had the night before. A glowing white figure, her long, almost silver hair framing a gentle face.

Before Verity could speak, Lizzy smiled and the lid of a wooden chest at her feet flipped open. Its contents flew up into the air as if caught in a whirlwind.

'Its contents flew up into the air as if caught in a whirlwind.'

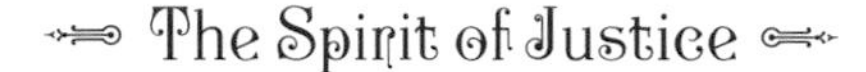

Verity looked around her in shock.

Hundreds of sheets of paper fluttered through the air like falling leaves.

Lizzy pointed at Verity's feet where a piece of faded paper had to come to rest.

Verity crouched down to pick it up. It showed part of a drawing. The right-hand side had been neatly torn away, but Verity recognized what remained. It was a plan for the construction of Traitor's Bridge.

Suddenly the attic was plunged into darkness. When Verity looked up, she found Lizzy had slipped away once more.

Verity sat up in bed until almost dawn, studying the plan of the bridge. "It must mean something," she muttered.

She thought back to the night before, when

Lizzy pointed across the river. She felt sure the ghost was relying on Verity to reveal the truth of her death.

But how did Lizzy die?

Perhaps if she put herself in Lizzy's place and re-enacted the events of that night, she might discover the answer…

That evening, Verity slipped from the house and headed for the stables. With trembling hands, she saddled her horse, Blaze, and led him from his stall until they were out of sight of the grooms' lodge.

Then she swung onto his back and rode down to the riverbank, just as Lizzy must surely have done on that fateful evening. All the while, Verity looked and listened for some sign, some hint of anything that might help her to make sense of what had happened.

At Traitor's Bridge, the only logical thing seemed to be to cross it. Blaze stepped onto the bridge gingerly, seeming to sense that a misstep could send them plummeting over the railings and into the Wilde.

As they reached the middle, Blaze felt confident enough to walk a little faster.

Verity had just begun to wonder what she would do when she reached the far side, when there was a loud creak and she felt Blaze rear up.

Verity gripped the reins in fright.

"What is it Blaze?" she cried.

In a split second, she realized that the bridge had collapsed underneath them. But before they had time to react, horse and rider were plunged into the swirling river.

"Help!" screamed Verity, as her head sank briefly beneath the surface.

Dirty river water filled her mouth. She was vaguely aware of Blaze making for the riverbank, and thrashed around, in a panic-stricken attempt to reach his bridle or even his mane.

The cold water chilled her as she desperately tried to stay afloat. And then something tugged at her elbows.

Whatever it was tightened its grip, and the next thing she knew, her head and shoulders were being lifted clear from the surface.

Gasping for breath and blinking water from her eyes, Verity found herself being towed across the river.

Looking up, she saw Lizzy's familiar white figure hovering just above the surface, her long dress fluttering in the night breeze.

Verity must have blacked out, for the next thing she knew, she was lying on a small stretch of earth, hidden from view beneath the bridge where it met the riverbank.

Choking from her ordeal, Verity pulled the sodden hair from her face and looked around for Lizzy's ghost. But her rescuer was nowhere to be seen.

Verity looked across the river, expecting to see the broken section of bridge dangling in the water. To her surprise, the bridge looked fine.

As she got to her feet, she noticed a circle of metal attached to the underside of the bridge above her head. A thick chain ran from it, along the length of the bridge. Further down, were what appeared to be levers.

Studying the mechanism more closely, Verity had an idea. If she was right, it would explain everything…

She heard a whinnying above her and saw Blaze on the riverbank, obviously shaken but otherwise as lively as ever.

Tugging at the folds of her wringing wet dress, she scrambled up the slope and led Blaze back to the house. She was greeted by her relieved parents, who had been on the point of sending out a search party.

Without mentioning Lizzy's ghost, Verity explained how she had re-enacted the events of that fateful night.

"I must rouse the Head Groundsman and get him to cordon off the bridge until it can be repaired," declared her father.

"It doesn't need repairing," said Verity. "But it may need to be made safe."

"What do you mean?" asked Verity's mother.

"I think Hugo Whitlock was responsible for Lizzy's death," said Verity. "Not to mention every servant he forced to cross Traitor's Bridge."

Sure enough, an inspection of the area beneath the bridge revealed a fiendishly cunning mechanism. When activated, it would cause a section of the bridge to collapse, tipping a horse and rider into the river, before returning to its normal position.

The remains of its victims, their canvas sacks lined with heavy weights, were an even more gruesome discovery.

"What a tragic series of events," sighed Verity's grandmother, as they walked by the river a few days later.

"I suppose Hugo must have forgotten to make the bridge safe again after his groom, Kendrick, went across the night before," said Verity.

Her grandmother nodded. "Hugo was accidentally responsible for his own daughter's death as a result. So of course he could never tell anyone what really happened."

"At least I've managed to clear Ben Mortimer's name," said Verity.

"Well that's what Lizzy wanted you to do," said her grandmother.

Verity shot her a look of surprise.

"She came to me too, many years ago," her grandmother went on, "but I was too scared or foolish to realize what she wanted."

Verity felt such a rush of relief that she immediately poured out every detail of her encounters with Lizzy's ghost. "But how was the bridge trap set again on the very night I went across?" she mused.

"Oh, I would have thought that was obvious," said her grandmother. "Lizzy, or rather her spirit, was responsible. It was the only way she could show you what had happened to her. And of course she knew she'd be on hand to pull you to safety."

Verity linked her arm with her grandmother's, and rested her head on her shoulder. She smiled to herself, sure in the knowledge that Lizzy Whitlock and all those unlucky servants were finally at peace.

The Lady in the Red Beret

"This station is now closed. This station is now closed!" boomed the announcement as Tarek hurtled through the gates to the underground station. The attendant was just about to shut them.

"But it says on the departures board that there's a train leaving in one minute!" Tarek pleaded. "Can I run down and try to catch it?"

"You can try, sonny," replied the attendant. "But you'll never make it in time..." he added, although Tarek barely heard him as he sprinted past. "And a Happy New Year to you, too!" muttered the attendant, grumpily.

Tarek ran down the escalator, his feet clacking against the metal as he went. As he leaped off the final couple of steps, he could see the train at the end of the passage ahead. Just then, he heard the driver's announcement.

"Please mind the doors, mind the closing doors now..."

He tore towards the platform as fast as he could, but it was no good.

Peeppeeppeeppeep! went the doors as they slammed shut in front of him.

The wheels whirred, and the train pulled away

into the darkness. Exhausted, Tarek slumped onto a bench to catch his breath.

The few people who had got off the train headed towards the exit. Tarek sighed. He'd missed the last train home. He pulled himself to his feet and was trudging back to the escalator, when something unexpected happened.

First, there was a faint hum in the distance, which slowly grew louder. Then, a gust of icy wind blew up, rustling discarded newspapers and sending a chilling whistle along the platform. A couple of thin brown mice scuttled past, squeaking.

The hum became a roar and then, to Tarek's amazement, another train came thundering into the station.

That's odd, thought Tarek, *I wonder why this one isn't up on the board...*

Even stranger was the fact that every single carriage was empty. Tarek hadn't even noticed a driver in the cab at the front. But he had just joined a newspaper as their most junior reporter, and he was incredibly curious by nature. He was determined to find out more about this mysterious train.

"It did say it's going to the right place on the front, so what's the harm in getting on?" he asked himself.

The doors slid open and bright carriage lights flooded out in front of him. He paused.

Something didn't seem quite right, but the train was there and if he didn't catch it, he faced a long, bitterly cold walk home.

With a shrug, he stepped into the empty carriage and the doors closed behind him. The train pulled out of the station and rattled into the dark tunnel ahead. Tarek settled down into a seat and then blinked as the lights started flickering on and off.

"It's just an ancient train," Tarek reassured himself, though he was beginning to feel a little on edge.

He looked down the length of the carriage, wondering if it was only a problem with the lights near his seat. What he saw next made the hairs on the back of his neck stand up.

Standing by the door further down the

'Standing by the door further down the carriage was a beautiful young woman.'

carriage was a beautiful young woman. She had flowing chestnut brown hair, and was wearing an old-fashioned coat with a matching raspberry red beret.

But there wasn't anybody in here a minute ago...

Suddenly, with Tarek's gaze fixed on the woman, the whole carriage was plunged into darkness. A second later, the lights came quivering back on and...

"She's disappeared!" Tarek gasped, staring in astonishment at the space where she had been. "What's going on?" he wondered aloud, standing up and heading down the carriage. He walked all the way to the end but there was no sign of the woman anywhere.

A loud screech from the brakes pierced the air as the train slowed down sharply. Tarek turned to go back to his seat and saw the woman again. She was standing right where he had been sitting.

But… but… that's impossible!

The train came into the next station and shuddered to a halt. The woman glanced up at Tarek, her shining green eyes momentarily meeting his, which were opened wide in amazement. She smiled gracefully, and stepped from the train.

Tarek was rooted to the spot, baffled by what he'd just seen.

He was shaken from his daze the moment the doors began to judder shut, and thrust his leg out to stop them from closing.

"Please wait!" he called after her.

Tarek hurried off the train and onto the escalator, bounding up two steps at a time in

an effort to catch up with the woman.

She must be here, he thought, as he tore into the empty ticket hall at the top and out to the exit.

He looked up and down the street both ways, but there was no one to be seen. Tarek couldn't understand it. Where could she have gone? She had simply vanished.

I'd better start walking home, he thought, with a sigh. *Nobody's ever going to believe this...*

"Yeah, yeah, very funny, Tarek. Pull the other one!" said his younger brother, the next day.

"Come on darling, stop it," added his mother,

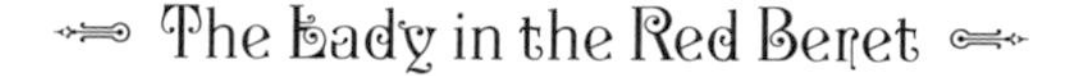

with his youngest sister looking worried beside her. "You're scaring Yasmin."

His friends, meanwhile, couldn't help but see the funny side. "You expect me to believe you saw a 'ghost' on the train on New Year's Eve? It was probably just someone playing around," said his best friend, Ali.

"Woooooo!" mocked Dave, pulling his white t-shirt over his head. "I'm Deathly Daaaaave. Now stop fooling around or I'll be forced to carry on haunting youuuu..."

But Tarek was sure of what he had seen, and he was determined to prove it, even if only to himself. Back at work, the first thing he did was to scour the newspaper archives to see if he could find anything useful.

He started by searching for 'New Year's Eve,

Underground' on his office computer. 'About 15,200,000 results' showed up on the screen, covering everything from parties to the last trains home.

Hmm... he thought, *maybe I should try being more specific.* And he entered 'New Year's Eve, Dalton Street station, young woman'. He paused for a second, then added, 'red beret'.

Two results flashed up.

Intrigued, he clicked on the first one, from a newspaper report dated January 1st 1933.

Heroic woman dies in tragic accident on New Year's Eve

A young woman of around 25 years of age fell under a train at Dalton Street station yesterday. Eyewitnesses said that she died a heroine, risking her own life to lift a stricken child off the tracks as the train approached.

"One minute everything was fine, then I think the little boy must have got too close to the platform edge and tumbled over. A young woman in a red beret jumped onto the tracks to rescue him, but she simply couldn't get herself back up in time," said a man who was at the scene.

The woman had been on her way to a New Year's Eve party when the tragedy happened.

Poor woman, thought Tarek.

He clicked on the second article. This was much more recent, from only a few years ago.

New Year's Eve Miracle at Dalton Street

A tragic accident was averted at the last moment yesterday evening, when a buggy

> blown towards the tracks miraculously stopped on the platform edge.
>
> One eyewitness said, "It was almost as if an invisible hand reached out and stopped it from falling." Then she smiled and added, "But I'm being fanciful. It was obviously just the wind that stopped it."

At the bottom of the article was a video captioned, 'The Dalton Street Miracle, caught live on CCTV.'

Tarek watched the clip and saw how the buggy had stopped only just in time. But he soon became more interested in a faint figure in the background. At first, she was standing on the stairs looking over the crowds. Then, as the buggy started moving towards the platform edge, she headed quickly to the platform, so quickly she could hardly be seen. In less than a second, she was heading back to the stairs, passing behind a small cluster of passengers. When they moved on, she had vanished.

Tarek replayed the clip to be sure. There was no doubt about it, even on the blurry security camera footage.

He could just make out her long brown hair, old-fashioned winter coat, and raspberry red beret…

"It was her!" he gasped.

After that, whenever Tarek went to Dalton Street station, he kept an eye out for the woman in the red beret.

Sometimes – and always on New Year's Eve – he thought he caught a glimpse of her, but in the blink of an eye, she would vanish. Still, she had that same kind smile on her face, as she watched over the crowds, making sure that every single single passenger got home safely.

The Emerald Ring

The events I am about to relate took place many years ago. I was just a young girl, and knew little of the world beyond my father's castle. What happened then seemed incredible. Now, as I finally scratch these words in black ink onto smooth parchment, it seems miraculous.

It was New Year, a time of feasting and revelry to cheer the coldest, darkest hours of winter.

After dinner in the Great Hall – a fine affair in those days, with roast meats, great pies and puddings aplenty – the tables were cleared away and the whole company gathered around the fire where the great Yule log crackled and spat.

Sometimes, a minstrel sang stories of brave deeds long ago, accompanying himself with quick fingers on his lute. Sometimes, my tutor read aloud from a vast book filled with stories of far-off lands. But that night, we had only plain tales told by the company, each taking a turn, and, for the first time I could recall, my father himself came forth to relate a tale.

"I tell you this story," he began, "because it concerns the fortune of my house and line. Listen well. It happened in the time of my youth, when I was journeying as a pilgrim to the shrine

housing the mortal remains of the holy lady Saint Winifred.

Near evening, I found myself riding across a wild stretch of moor. I was alone, having sent my squire on ahead to the next town to find a place to stay. As twilight fell, my horse faltered and whinnied nervously, flattening its ears and refusing to walk on.

Wondering what could be the matter, I peered through the gloom and saw a hooded figure standing at the side of the road. As I watched, the figure slowly put up a hand and pushed back the hood, revealing the gaunt, pinched features of an old woman.

Her cloak was so ragged, I knew her station in life must be very humble. Although night was rapidly falling, it was as if a strange light fell about her, as I could see her quite clearly. Her hair was white and her skin wrinkled, but her eyes were ageless and shining, looking straight at me with keen interest.

I urged my horse on, but still it refused. Puzzled, I dismounted and went forward on foot, leading my horse, which followed, though unwillingly. As I drew closer, the woman called out in a high, clear voice.

'Please, sire, spare some charity for a poor creature fallen on hard times!'

I heard such requests almost every day, but

whether it was the twilight, or the lonely place, or something in the old woman's shining eyes, her words seemed to pierce my very heart.

Immediately, I felt at my belt for my purse. My hand met empty air. I had given the purse to my squire to pay for that night's food and lodging. But the woman's words resounded in my brain, and I knew I must help her. Quickly, I slipped from my finger a fine gold ring set with an emerald. 'Good woman,' I said, 'I have no coins, but please accept this ring. May it bring you to better fortune.'

I held out the ring, and as the woman took it, the gold band and the green stone set into it shone strangely in the light that seemed to cling about her. She looked at the ring, and then gave me a long, searching look.

'It is a noble gift, sire,' she said. 'You are truly a good man.' And she turned, raised her hood and seemed to glide off, with surprising speed for one so old, disappearing into the blackness.

All at once, I felt terribly weary and alone. But my horse seemed to have recovered so I remounted and set off once more. Soon I was warming myself by the fire of the inn in the next village, where I found my squire. We spent the evening in merry company, though my thoughts kept straying back to the old woman I had met on my way.

That night, in the small hours, as I lay somewhere between sleeping and waking, I was abruptly gripped by cold, and observed a pale, glimmering light. Looking across the room, I saw a vision I have never forgotten.

'The same strange radiance shone about her face, illuminating the whole chamber.'

There was my squire, sleeping soundly at the foot of the bed, but standing nearby, wearing her shabby cloak, I was astonished to see the old woman. The same strange radiance shone about her face, illuminating the whole chamber.

'Sir William,' she said, her voice clear and strong, 'you showed me true charity. Know that I am Saint Winifred. Now, I return your ring to you. Keep it safe in memory of me.

As long as you have the ring, it will bring you and your heirs good fortune, just as you wished good fortune on me.'

Before I could move or speak, the room was plunged into blackness, I felt myself falling back and knew no more.

The following morning, as soon as I woke, I questioned my squire, but the boy had slept deeply all night. I leaned back on the bed in puzzlement, and saw a glint of gold and green as the ring tumbled out from under my pillow.

From that day forth I treasured the ring, placing it in a casket inscribed on the lid with the name of Saint Winifred and keeping it hidden in the deep vaults under this castle. And, until today, I have never told this tale to any soul, save one."

Here my father paused, and gave a deep sigh.

"You all know that my dear son, Hugh, was made a knight by the King's own hand a year ago. He was always a headstrong boy, but the day he rode off to the wars I judged that the time had come to entrust him with the story.

I took him to the vaults in secret and showed him the ring, telling him of the blessing the saint had bestowed, as long as the ring was kept safe in her memory. I little knew then what would happen.

The very next day, my steward brought me the terrible news. Checking the vaults during his daily rounds, he had found the casket lying on the floor: empty. The ring was gone.

The pain this loss caused me was doubled, knowing that the saint's blessing was now withdrawn, and that my dearest son must be to blame. Since then I have counted the days, waiting for misfortune to strike. I fear it is no mere chance that Hugh has failed to return from the wars, when so many others are safely home. Surely the saint has chosen to punish the

one who took her ring so heedlessly."

My father sat down and stared sadly into the fire, but my mother got up and hurried from the Hall. The company scattered, murmuring good nights, and I was led away by my nurse. My father stayed, staring at the flames, with only his steward, standing stiffly at his side, for company.

That night, as I lay in bed, I pondered on my father's words.

Hugh had always been strong-willed, it is true. But he had a kind, open nature and I could not believe that he would take anything in secret. What could a girl of ten years do, in any case, when even the lord of the castle was at a loss? I wondered over and over what had happened to the ring, and eventually fell into a restless sleep.

I do not know how long I dozed, but I awoke

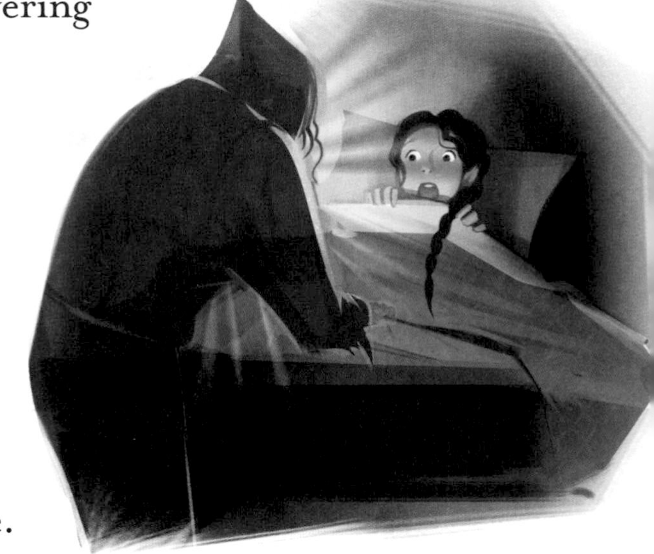

with a start, shivering with cold. A chill, blue light seemed to fill the room and I looked up in terror as a hooded figure loomed over me.

I tried to cry out, but my throat seized up with fear and no sound came. I saw a hand go up and push back the threadbare hood, and my fear turned to wonder. The face I saw was pale, lined and thin, but it gave off an unearthly radiance, and kindness shone from the eyes. I knew this must be Saint Winifred, just as my father had described her.

"Do you know who I am?" she asked, in clear tones that sent shivers through my whole body.

I managed to nod my head.

"You are right to believe in your brother's innocence. Do you wish to help him?"

Again, I nodded.

"Find the ring." The saint's voice was urgent. "Your father has failed in his task to keep the ring safe in my memory. It has been taken by someone who does not respect me, and he means to sell it soon for a handful of coins. He has hidden it in the castle garden. You will know where to look."

I stared at her, confused, but the light about her was fading fast as she drew up her hood. Questions raced through my mind, but already I felt the heaviness of sleep overwhelm me as my head fell slowly back onto my pillow. That was the last thing I remembered.

When I woke, my small room was filled with light and I looked around wildly, thinking the saint was still there… until I realized it was morning. I ran to my nurse and poured out the whole tale, begging her to come with me to search for the ring. But she would not listen.

"You poor child!" she exclaimed. "That story last night was too much for you. What dreams you have been having. You must keep to your room today. I will bring you a soothing drink."

I argued and protested in vain. All day I paced my room, but evening came and I was no closer to finding the ring.

I slept fitfully that night, and woke with a start to find the strange, pale radiance bathing the room once more. Looking up in alarm, I saw the ragged figure standing at the foot of the bed, just as she had the night before. Once more she spoke to me, but this time her voice sounded harsh and reproachful, and her words burned into my brain.

"Did you not heed my warning? Misfortune will come to your family swiftly if the ring is not found. You *must* find it. It is in the garden. You will know where to look."

Afraid though I was, I struggled to speak, to ask her what she meant. But, again, sleep and darkness swiftly overcame me.

The next day, I awoke with the saint's words still echoing in my mind, and desperately pleaded with my nurse.

"You must help me," I begged her. "The ring

is in the garden somewhere. I need to find it!"

She simply gave me a worried look. "Hush, child!" she soothed, "You need to rest. Another day indoors won't harm you."

I could have shouted with frustration, but I knew it would not help. Powerless, I stared out of the window at the castle garden, and the saint's words came back to me: "You will know where to look." *What could she mean?*

All day in my chamber I turned it over in my mind, thinking of the summer games I played with the squires and pages in the castle garden: blind man's buff, tag, hunt the thimble... I dragged my mind back to the last time we had played. It was the end of the summer, and we had annoyed my father's steward as he sat reading in a corner of the garden. He watched with a sour face as I tucked the thimble into a hole in the trunk of an apple tree. But how could that help me now?

By the end of the day, I was just as puzzled, and dreaded what the night might bring. The saint would be really angry now that I had failed her, as well as my father. "I *will* stay awake!" I told myself as I lay there yawning in the dark. And then suddenly, puzzling it over in the blackness, I understood. *The hole in the apple tree — that must be where the ring was hidden.* I had found the answer! Relief flooded through me and I fell instantly into a restful sleep.

That night, nothing disturbed my slumbers. In the morning, my nurse seemed satisfied I had slept well, and I waited patiently as she fastened my sleeves and braided my hair. As soon as she let me, I slipped out of the room, and ran through the dark passageways of the castle, down to the garden gate. It was a chill and rainy day and I shivered as I ran across the wet grass of the garden. I reached up to the hole in the tree trunk, then paused, almost fearing to find out the truth.

At that moment, my father and the steward came into view, talking busily together, and I knew I had to act swiftly. I plunged in my hand and my fingers closed over cold metal.

Before I could move or speak, the steward looked at me, gave a cry, then ran, stumbling, towards the gatehouse. My father stared after him in astonishment, then spun around to me. I held out my hand. There, among some scraps of dead leaf curled and crumbling like old parchment, the emerald ring glinted green and gold.

My father's face changed from bewilderment to joy, then quickly darkened with sorrow. "So my steward overheard us, stole the ring and blamed it on Hugh!" he murmured.

"How could I have believed in him, and not in my own son?" He held me close as I told him my tale of night visitations from Saint Winifred.

"The good saint be praised!" he cried, "Through you, in her wisdom, she has restored your brother's good name."

That night in the Great Hall he told the tale to all the company. He had barely ceased when a noise was heard outside, and a servant ran in, bringing urgent news.

"It's your son, my lord," he cried, "returned from the wars!"

Great was the rejoicing with Hugh that night. When I was finally sent to bed, I lay down in true contentment, my duty done. But, later that night, I woke once more shivering with cold.

There stood Saint Winifred, in the same cloak

and with the same pale light falling from her. This time she was smiling.

"You have done well," she said, "But I ask one thing more of you. Write this down, so your descendants may know of it in years to come."

Pulling up her hood, she vanished, leaving me staring into the black space where she had been.

Never again did the holy lady visit me, and as the years passed I often meant to write of her. It is hard to find the words for such strange deeds. But now, at last, at the end of my life, I have done so, and this is the tale you have read.

Smoke and Mirrors

The stage curtain peeled open, and the lights dimmed to a dull orange glow. I shifted in my seat, struggling to see between the heads of the audience. Everyone fell silent. There was no music or flashing lights as in other magic shows I'd watched. As the curtain drew wider, all I saw was pale smoke wafting around the stage, like an early morning mist. The smoke began to swirl and twist, making shapes. The cloud parted and then I saw him: *the magician.*

The Great Mephisto sat on a chair in the middle of the stage, his head hanging to one side. He was a strange-looking man, entirely hairless and as pale as the moon, except for a jagged red scar that ran down his right cheek. He didn't move, not an inch.

"He's nodded off!" one of the audience laughed. "In his own magic show!"

There were a few laughs, but I knew the magician wasn't sleeping.

"What's happening?" said my sister beside me.

"I think he's in a trance," I breathed.

The smoke began to gather into a dark globe, directly above the Great Mephisto. Now the globe started to spin, like a whirlwind, so fast it sent a rush of wind across the audience. One man yelped as his wig blew from his head, but no one paid him any attention. Our eyes were fixed on the stage.

A tendril of smoke uncoiled from the globe. As it reached out towards the audience, something like fingers flexed on its end.

No, not something *like* fingers. They *were* fingers. It was an arm.

Another arm formed. Slowly the smoke took the vague shape of a person. It was wispy and blurred, but definitely a person.

"It's the Spirit!" someone cried.

"The Screaming Spirit!" came a shriek.

This was the trick we'd been waiting for. It was the Great Mephisto's most famous act: the Screaming Spirit.

The spirit hung in the air above the magician, drifting gently back and forth, its cloudy head flopped low in front of its chest.

And then the head rose.

I gripped my sister's arm, chilled to the bone by what I saw. Its eyes… They were like black holes, swirling, growing larger, a glowing pupil in the middle of each. I was convinced they were staring straight at me. I wanted to scream, but I could hardly even breathe.

The only sound came from the spirit. Its mouth yawned open, and a cry came out unlike any I'd ever heard – a vicious, screeching sound, like shattering glass. Now I screamed too. My sister screamed. Everyone in the place screamed.

The stage curtain fell.

The main lights flickered on, and the screams turned into relieved laughter.

The curtain rose again. The Great Mephisto,

'Its eyes... were like black holes... a glowing pupil in the middle of each.'

now wide awake, stood at the front of the stage. His face was flushed, with ruby cheeks and twinkling emerald eyes. All of the smoke, every wisp of it, had vanished.

The scar gleamed on the magician's face as he rose from a bow, and everyone burst into thunderous applause. Everyone, that is, except me. I just sat there, stunned.

I was much younger than most people there, but I'd seen a lot of magic shows. I love magic. It's my hobby. I'm only a beginner but I can do some good tricks with cards and coins. And I really love *watching* magic. Each year for my birthday my older sister takes me to see a show. She'd saved up for weeks for tickets to the Great Mephisto, but it had been worth every penny. His tricks were incredible.

Only…

That *last* trick. The Screaming Spirit.

It had seemed so real…

As we headed for home, my sister noticed the look on my face; stunned, as if I'd been slapped. She squeezed my shoulder and smiled. "Remember what Dad used to say. It's all just smoke and mirrors," she said.

My dad did always say that about magic – *just smoke and mirrors.* He was right. Most magicians use smoke machines, cleverly positioned mirrors, trapdoors and other props to make their tricks seem real. But, no matter how hard I thought about it, I couldn't see how the Screaming Spirit could be a trick.

I'd always dreamed there might be such a thing as *real* magic, a world of spirits and spells. My dad died over a year ago. He'd introduced me to magic. He loved it too. Some nights, when I couldn't sleep from how much I missed him, I prayed that I could see or talk to him again. I was desperate to know he was still there; that magic was real.

That evening, for the first time, I felt as if I'd looked into that magical world. It had looked back, too – and screamed.

No, I was being silly. My dad was right. It was all just smoke and mirrors. *Wasn't it?*

That night I saw the Screaming Spirit in my dream. I woke up crying and soaked with sweat. But I didn't tell anyone about the nightmare. I was scared they'd stop me from watching magic.

The next morning I looked through my magic books. Like I said, I'm obsessed with magic, and have loads of books about it. Some teach tricks, but others are about the history of magic and the lives of magicians. I read about stage illusions and acts with smoke and mirrors. But, still, I couldn't solve how the Great Mephisto had performed the Screaming Spirit. I couldn't get rid of the chill inside me.

Things got even stranger when I opened the oldest book in my collection, a dusty history of magic I'd found in a second-hand bookshop. It mentioned a magician called the Magnificent Carter, who had tried to perform a ghost trick. Only, the act had gone badly wrong and he was laughed off stage.

Carter never performed again, and died shortly after that show. That was over fifty years ago though. I doubted Carter's ghost trick was the same as the Great Mephisto's.

I was about to put the book down when I stopped and looked again.

There was a small photo of the Magnificent Carter. He was young and good-looking, with dark hair tied in a pony tail. A long jagged scar ran down his right cheek.

My grip tightened on the book. I leaned closer, making sure I'd seen correctly.

I had.

It was the same scar I'd seen on the Great Mephisto the day before.

I rushed downstairs to our computer, and looked up a photo of the Great Mephisto. The scar was *exactly* the same.

Carter had hair while the Great Mephisto was bald, but otherwise... They were one and the same person.

I didn't simply feel a chill now. My insides had turned to ice. Was it possible that the Magnificent Carter was now the Great Mephisto, performing the same trick? It couldn't be. The book said Carter had died fifty years ago. And, anyway, his version of the ghost trick was so bad he'd been laughed off stage.

I tried to laugh too, to convince myself I was being silly. But it came out weak and hollow. Something strange was going on. Something, maybe, more than a trick.

The house was empty, so I couldn't show anyone the pictures. Besides, I was determined to find out for myself. The Great Mephisto was giving another performance that afternoon. There was no way I could afford a ticket, but I didn't want to see the show again anyway. I wanted to see *behind* the show.

I grabbed my coat and set off.

I ran all the way to the playhouse. Even from outside I could hear the audience clap and cheer. The show was well underway.

Gathering my nerve, I darted down an alley to the back of the building. There was only one door and it was locked. That didn't bother me. One of the first tricks my dad taught me was how to pick a lock. I brought out the slim steel lock pick I always carry in my sock, and in no time the door was open.

I crept inside. It was only early afternoon, but the corridor was as dark as midnight. It was eerily quiet too. I could just hear a murmur of chattering voices, and realized it was the audience. The show had entered the interval.

But there was no noise backstage. It didn't make sense. My dad had told me that backstage at a magic show was always a buzzy, busy place. The Great Mephisto's assistants should have been rushing around, preparing the stage for his final act, the Screaming Spirit.

Yet there was no one here. It was as if the magician *had* no assistants or props.

Behind me, something moved.

I turned, but all I saw was the door creaking in the wind.

"Hello?" I hissed.

A cold breeze swept along the corridor, though that wasn't why I shivered.

Suddenly I didn't want to be there.

Another breeze rustled my hair, carrying with it a wisp of smoke. It rushed past and the door behind me slammed shut.

I ran back, tried to pull it open.

Locked?

But no one had been there! I tried my lock pick again, but my hand was shaking with fear. I couldn't open the door.

The only way was forward.

I kept moving, towards the sound of the audience's voices. My eyes had adjusted better to the dark. I could see that there was only one door off the corridor, and it was open.

As I edged closer, another twist of smoke floated from the room beyond. It rose and turned, as if it was glancing around the gloom.

All at once, it shot back inside.

I'd never been so scared in my life. But, at the same time, I'd never felt so determined. *What was going on here?*

I crept on, closer to the open door. Another line of smoke slid through the gap, this time along the floor like some monstrous slug. Just as quickly, it retreated back inside.

The air grew colder, and goose bumps prickled my arms. I breathed in deeply, and stepped into the room.

A single candle burned in one corner. Its soft

glow fell on a sofa, and on the sofa was the Great Mephisto himself.

The magician lay on his back, his arms crossed over his chest. The scar on his cheek glistened in the candlelight, but his skin was pale.

"Hello?" I said, stepping nearer.

The magician didn't move.

I went nearer still.

I reached a shaky hand, touched his cheek below the scar. His skin was ice cold.

"No..." I gasped.

I rested a hand on his chest. He wasn't breathing. The Great Mephisto was dead.

I knew then that this was the Magnificent Carter, and he *had* died. He was haunted by his own ghost, using it to perform the trick under a new name, the Great Mephisto. It was a trick

he'd been mocked for once, but had now mastered – a ghost trick with a real ghost. His *own* ghost.

It was true.

It was all true...

But if the spirit wasn't inside him now, where was it?

"You know my secret," a voice said.

It was like a voice from a grave, deep and filled with death. It came from behind me.

At first I couldn't move, my legs were so heavy with fear. Then, very slowly, I turned.

The spirit hovered in the air, its black eyes swirling, the pupils boring into me.

I gripped the edge of the sofa, holding myself steady.

"Why have you come here?" the spirit said.

"I... I wanted to know if it was real."

"Real?"

"Magic. That magic can be real."

The spirit's mouth opened… and what came out surprised me. It wasn't a scream, but a laugh, deep and booming, like distant thunder.

Suddenly, the spirit rushed at me. I covered my face and screamed as the ghost shot right through me. It felt like ice – as if my whole body briefly turned to ice.

When I looked again, the spirit was gone.

The Great Mephisto sat up on the sofa. He looked alive and well again, a flush on his face, the sparkle back in his eyes. He stretched his arms, clicking their joints.

"And now that you know about magic," he said at last, "how do you feel?"

"I want to know more," I replied, sounding braver than I felt.

He considered my answer for a long moment, stroking his scar with a single finger. Then he rose, walked right past me and out of the door. "My audience is waiting," he said.

I rushed after him. The cold inside me was replaced with fire. Tears welled in my eyes, but I fought them back. "Tell me!" I demanded. "Tell me how I can learn more about your world."

He stopped, turned. His face darkened and his voice deepened. It was the spirit's voice.

"You must find out for yourself, as I did. You will make a fine magician, Samuel. Perhaps the finest. But be careful. You are right. There is life beyond life. There is death beyond death. The more you enter that world, Samuel, the more you may know its terrors. But it holds beauty too, and sadness and great, great joy."

He continued walking.

"Wait!" I cried. "How... How do you know my name?"

I hadn't told him. I hadn't mentioned it at all.

The magician stopped, but didn't turn. His voice was warm again, and I sensed that he was smiling. "Your father told me," he said. "He is right behind you."

I whirled around, but saw nothing except the door to the outside, now wide open. I turned back, and the Great Mephisto was gone too. I heard the audience gasp and scream as he performed his final act, the Screaming Spirit.

No one saw me as I sank down against the wall. And no one heard me as my tears finally came out in gasping, gulping sobs.

I gazed around the corridor through blurred watery eyes.

"Dad?" I asked. "Dad, are you here?"

The door creaked open wider.

"I miss you," I said. "We all miss you… so very much."

The door slammed shut.

"But I know now that you were wrong. It's not all just smoke and mirrors. You *are* there…

I know you're there."

The door opened again. Afternoon sun beamed in, flooding the corridor with light.

I had to leave. My sister would be home soon and she'd be worried.

I rose, feeling a little shaky, and put my hands against the wall, steadying myself.

As I left, the ground trembled from cheering and clapping and stomping feet.

The Great Mephisto's act was over.

But, for me, the show was just beginning.

Acknowledgements

Designed by Sam Whibley

Edited by Lesley Sims

Digital manipulation by John Russell

This is a work of fiction. The characters, incidents, and dialogues are products of the authors' imaginations and are not to be construed as real. Any resemblance to actual events or persons, living or dead, is entirely coincidental.

First published in 2015 by Usborne Publishing Ltd., 83-85 Saffron Hill, London EC1N 8RT, England. www.usborne.com